We're Going to

Hollywood !

Happy Reading!

by

Robert Lawrence Gilstrap

Robert Lawrence Gilstrap

PublishAmerica
Baltimore

First printing

ISBN: 1-4137-5378-7
PUBLISHED BY PUBLISHAMERICA, LLLP
www.publishamerica.com
Baltimore

Printed in the United States of America

Acknowledgments

To Kathryn Jenson Pierce, my instructor for
A Writing Books for Children: the Craft and the Market
my second course with the Institute for Children's Literature.

Patti Gilstrap, my daughter, and Patsy Harris, my sister,
who read the manuscript when it was ready to be shared.

To Dan Dailey, my friend, and Brian, his teenage son, who were my only
non-family member readers.

To Jeannette Gartrell and all the wonderful people
at Publish America who helped turn my first novel into a real book!

This book is dedicated to

Dorothy,
the love of my life,

and J.D. Gilstrap,
my father,

and Walter Barclay,
her father.

Other Books by the Robert Lawrence Gilstrap

The Sultan's Fool and Other North African Tales
with Irene Estabrook

Ten Texas Tales

New Land, New Lives
with Rembert Patrick

Current Strategies for Teachers
with William R. Martin

Ready to Read: A Parent's Guide
with Mary Ann Dzama

Author's Note

Several years before my father, J. D. Gilstrap, died of an aneurism, he sat on the glassed-in patio of his modest home in Marshall, Texas, and did a tape-recorded autobiography for me and my sister, Patsy, and our children and grandchildren. Although he was legally blind and had a severe hearing loss, my father had lived a good life, and he knew it. There had been many changes in his world since he was born on November 30, 1906, in East Texas. In his audio tape, he begins with his first memory when he was six years of age. This memory was the birth of his youngest brother, Sam, who almost died as an infant.

My father then describes the farm near Marshall where he lived and worked for almost seven years from ages six to thirteen. He had already done a watercolor painting of that farm which hangs in my kitchen. He also describes what it was like to go to the Farmers' Institute, which was five miles from the farm. He had painted a picture of this school at Bunker Hill which depicted him in 1913 with his syrup bucket lunch container in his hand, standing near a water well.

My father also describes seeing his first movie and his first non-farm job working in a silent movie theater selling tickets, painting posters, and running the player-piano rolls that accompanied the movies. He had left me and my sister a valuable gift through his taped autobiography and watercolors, and I wanted to get a similar record on tape before my mother died, but unfortunately I did not.

During a recent family reunion for my wife's family, my father-in-law, who was born on June 15, 1916, in Johnstown, Pennsylvania, began sharing some of his boyhood memories of growing up in Hollywood, California, where his father worked as a publicist for Samuel Goldwyn Studios, and his mother worked as an occasional extra during the silent movie period. He was even in a crowd scene in one of these old films and had seen some of the greats, such as Harold Lloyd, as they made some of their classic films.

After hearing of his fascinating boyhood, I asked him if he would do an audio-taped autobiography the next time we were together, and he agreed to do so. As I listened to my father-in-law's stories, the idea for this book emerged.

My idea was to share the boyhood of my father and the boyhood of my father-in-law with the children in our families and other young readers through a historical novel based on their tape-recorded autobiographies. The central character of this novel is thus a composite of both men.

Other characters in the book and incidents not mentioned in the tapes have been created to make the story of interest. My goal, however, is to help the reader learn more about this exciting time in the history of our nation when life and culture were transformed by the "movies" and the effect they had on one boy, J.W. Gilclay, and his family.

Robert Lawrence Gilstrap
Lake Monticello, Virginia

One

"J.W.! It's time for supper!"

I was out slopping the hogs when I heard my ma calling me. The big Texas sun was just beginning to set and I was sure getting hungry. I suppose that was not unusual for a thirteen-year-old boy who still had a lot of growing to do.

Papa and Ma kept me busy working on the farm all summer, but I didn't mind. They worked just as hard as me and my older brothers did. We grew mostly cotton, but we also planted a few watermelons each year.

I would soon be back in school and "hitting the books," as my papa said. My papa had not been able to finish high school, but learning to read and write was very important to him. That's why he encouraged me and the other kids to go to the Farmers' Institute, which was five miles away from our farm.

When I walked into the kitchen of our farm house, I could tell that Papa and Ma had been fussing with each other. Papa's face was red and Ma was wiping away tears. I sat across from my two older brothers, Don and Clifford, and between my younger brother, Sammy, and Baby Juanita.

"Let's thank the Lord for what we are about to receive," Papa said. "Amen."

We all said "amen" with Papa and then began to pass platters of food around. Ma had made potato pancakes and pork sausage for supper. We had finally eaten all of the spoiled sausage that I had ruined one day when I was on smokehouse duty. I had put a leather shoe in the fire instead of going out to get wood from the wood pile. Oh, that sausage tasted so terrible! But I never confessed to the family because I would have been teased without mercy by my older brothers.

Don would have thought it was funny for me to do something that didn't make sense, in hindsight. But Clifford would never had let me forget about it. He was always getting me in trouble at school anyway. When he did something bad, the teacher would whip us both. I didn't want him to have anything to tease me about at school. I might lose my temper and start swinging my lunch bucket at him. Then we'd all be expelled the way we were last year when I was in sixth grade. That's when Don, my oldest brother, yelled at the teacher for being mean to Sammy. My little brother was having trouble remembering a poem.

Nobody said a word as we ate supper and washed it down with cool buttermilk. Children were to be seen and not heard, unless spoken to by an adult. I loved potato pancakes and accepted a second helping when Ma asked if anyone still was hungry. I always said "yes" to seconds and sometimes asked if there were any biscuits or blackberry cobbler left from our big meal at noon. Blackberry cobbler was my favorite dessert, but biscuits filled with dark corn syrup could also be mighty tasty. That was usually our afternoon snack. We were always hungry after walking such a long distance from school.

Papa ate his food fast, as he normally did, and Ma took his plate away. She then brought him a cup of hot coffee without him even asking. She must have known that he was going out after supper. He sometimes drove his old wagon, pulled by the gray mule that helped him with the planting each spring.

He usually went to visit his pa and ma, who lived just about two miles away. Grandpa would always ask where the kids were, because he really liked to tease us. He would hear a dog yelping in the background and try to make us think that it was a wild cat.

I used to think that he was telling the truth and would run to Ma, crying like a baby. She would just laugh and so would Grandpa. Now the only one who really believes they are wildcats is Baby Juanita. I'm sure she will soon learn that Grandpa is just a big tease. That's why we like him so much.

"Kids," my father said after Ma sat down again. I've got something to tell you. Your mother and I have been counting the money we earned this summer, and the picture looks mighty grim. We didn't earn enough to pay our bills, much less make a payment on the mortgage."

Ma began to dab at her eyes with a handkerchief as Papa talked.

"I think you all know that your Grandpa helped us buy this farm by loaning us $450. That's a lot of money, and we agreed to pay him back as soon as we could. Last year, we raised enough food to feed our family and sold some cotton at the farmer's market so that we could buy stuff that we couldn't raise, like salt and sugar. But there was no money left for the mortgage payment. The same thing has happened this year."

"Was that because of all the rain we had in the spring, Pa?" Don asked.

I also wanted to know. We had all worked so hard that it was disappointing to hear Papa say that it had not been enough. My brothers and I had even taken some watermelons that didn't sell over to Grandpa's house on the big road. But nobody bought them because there were already so many other people selling watermelons. At the end of the day, we punched them open with our sweaty fists and ate the hearts out of each one. That was the last time we tried to be watermelon salesmen.

Papa had laughed when we told him our story, but I could tell that he was disappointed as well. Any extra money would have helped during such a rough year.

"The rain was part of the problem, Don," Papa said. "But the real problem is, I'm just not cut out to be a farmer like my daddy. After two years of busting my butt and having nothing to show for it, I'm ready to tell Grandpa to sell the farm to some man who can. We've all worked as hard as we can, and look what we have to show for it. I'm ready to move to Marshall and see if I can make some money working at the sawmill. At least I can make enough money there to support my family."

I could hardly believe what I was hearing. I couldn't believe my papa was going to give up being a farmer. I knew things had been tough, but I liked living on the farm better than any place my family had ever lived. Although we had to work hard, we had also had a lot of fun.

I remembered the time when Papa had bought a billy goat for the family. He let the boys use his tools to cut logs and build a wagon. That goat was the smelliest thing, but all of our friends wanted to come over and take a ride.

I would sure miss my best friend, Joseph, who lived with his family in the farm nearby. We loved to go fishing together whenever we had any spare time. And we talked about what we would do when we were grown up.

In fact, there was nothing about living on the farm that I didn't like, except walking ten miles to and from school. That would continue for a long time, until I finished eighth grade. I especially liked our Christmas celebrations when Papa chopped down a pine tree and put it next to the barn. Then the kids decorated it with popcorn and sang Christmas carols.

When night had come, we went inside the farm house to see what Santa Claus had brought us. It usually was an orange and an apple and a two-bit toy.

I could not remember a happier time than the years that we had spent on this farm. Why would anyone not want to live in this beautiful place surrounded by tall pine trees?

"Pa, I can't believe you're serious," I said with a lump in my throat. "This is a great place to live and we're all happy here. I'm sure next year will be better. Don and Cliff and I will do a better job of selling those watermelons."

"No, J.W. My mind is made up. I'm riding over in the wagon to see your grandpa and let him know my decision."

Papa got up from the table and left the farm house. Ma didn't kiss him goodbye the way she usually did. Pretty soon I could hear him take off in his wagon with his mule pulling him to Grandpa's farm.

The sun had set about an hour earlier. My body was beginning to feel sleepy after such a hard day of work in the summer heat. And my mind was still reeling with the thought of no longer being a farm boy and becoming a city slicker.

"Ma," I said. "I think I'll go to bed now. I'm really tired."

"I understand," Ma said. "Give me a kiss."

I thought I was too big to be giving Ma a goodnight kiss,

but I usually did anyway, when she asked. That was the least I could do for all the nice things she did for me.

When I went to the room where I slept with my three brothers, I could not go to sleep. I was too sad thinking about leaving the farm and moving to Marshall. I still felt like crying but knew that boys my age didn't do that. Instead I started thinking about what I could do to change Pa's mind.

Maybe Joseph could help me come up with an idea. I decided to go see him early the next morning. His father was having trouble paying his bills, too. World War I had just ended and it was still tough making a living in Texas during the summer of 1920. I was sure Joseph would be able to help. After all, he was my best friend.

 TWO

The next morning, the entire family was up early. It was another sunny and humid summer day. Papa and Ma called August a scorcher, and the month was definitely living up to their description.

After a big, country breakfast of fried eggs, sausage, hash-brown potatoes, and biscuits, I was out doing my chores with my brothers. Baby Juanita stayed inside with Ma. This summer I was big and strong enough to take care of the pigs and hogs, so that's what I did first.

As soon as the pigs saw me, they came squealing out to let me know that they were just as hungry as my family had been when we sat around our big pine table just minutes earlier. The hog pen was close to the barn, which was only a few yards from our small farm house. I quickly took care of feeding the hogs by giving them watermelon and ears of corn. They gobbled the food down greedily and then looked up for more.

We now had seven pigs, a sow, and a boar. I was responsible for keeping them fed during the spring, summer, and fall. Then when there was going to be four or five days of cold weather, it was hog-killing time.

Neighbors would come over and help us with the killing, and we would go to their farms to help them. After the hogs were slaughtered, Papa and Ma would salt them down and store them for about a week before putting them in the smokehouse where they would be cured.

Taking care of the hogs was very important to my family, and I took my job very seriously. If any of the pigs died, there would be less food on our table during the winter. That's just the way things were on a farm.

But that's what I liked about being a farm boy. I liked being outside most of the year and taking care of animals. That's why it was hard for me to be happy about Papa's plan to move back to Marshall. That's why I just had to do something to make him reconsider his decision.

"Papa, I finished feeding the pigs and hogs," I said. "May I go over to Joseph's farm and see if I can catch some catfish for dinner?"

The entire family loved catfish, but it was especially one of Papa's favorite foods. Ma would dip it in corn flour and fry it until it was crisp and golden brown. She'd then make some hush puppies and cole slaw, and we'd wash it all down with cool milk from our cow.

"That sounds mighty good to me, J.W.," Papa replied. "Just come home for dinner even if you don't catch anything. The sun's mighty hot, and I don't want you having a heat stroke like Don almost did last week."

Although Papa could sometimes be a grouch, he really loved us kids and wanted what was best for us. He seemed in a much better mood than the previous night when he was telling us about his plans to move back to Marshall.

"Sure, Papa," I said as I took a cane fishing pole from

behind our house. We kept three poles there for any member of the family who might want to go fishing.

Joseph's farm was about three miles from ours, so I was there in less than an hour. I ran part of the way because I was so anxious to talk to him and to see if he had any suggestions for me about how I might convince my papa to stay on the farm for at least another year.

I had only known Joseph since I was about eleven. We met at the county fair. Both of our families were there enjoying the sights and sounds of this annual event. I had never been to anything like it before, but Joseph, who was a year older, had been several times.

One of the highlights of the fair for me was seeing my first moving picture. I don't know what the name of it was, but it was really exciting. Some men in hot air balloons were having a race and one man kept doing things to make the other man lose. My family and I sat in the dark on the grass and some man projected an image on a white sheet that had been hung between two tall pine trees.

There was a tall boy with bright-orange hair in front of me who kept jumping up and down with excitement. I remember being annoyed by him and told him to sit down so we could see the movie.

When he turned around to say something to me, I saw one of the friendliest freckle-covered faces I have ever seen. Wearing a big smile, he asked me if I wanted to sit on the grass in front of him so I could see better. I said yes.

After the movie, he told me that his name was Joseph and that he lived near my farm.

When school began in the fall, Joseph and I got to know each other even better. He walked with me and my family home each day and always had something funny to say about our teacher, Mr. Haggard, who sometimes did things that could be very annoying. One day the teacher found a love note that Cliff had written to a girl in the class and read it aloud to everybody. Joseph wondered if anyone had ever been in love with Mr. Haggard. We all found it hard to imagine him kissing anyone. As we walked through the woods, Joseph pretended to be Mr. Haggard kissing and hugging his girlfriend in the form of a tree. He made us all laugh as we walked home from school.

Joseph also liked to play baseball, a game that we would sometimes play after eating our noon meal. He had made a ball out of string and another boy had made a bat with his father's help.

When I finally got to Joseph's house, I did not see him anyplace. I saw his ma, however, out in the back of the house washing clothes. She had heated water in a big black kettle and was stirring the dirty clothes 'round and 'round until the dirt came out of them.

"Hi, J.W.," Mrs. Glenn said to me. "Looking for Joseph?"

"I sure am," I replied. "I'm hoping I can talk him into going fishing with me. My family's getting hungry for catfish."

"I think he's in the barn," Mrs. Glenn explained.

When I went into the barn, I saw that Joseph' s ma was correct. I found Joseph and his pa leaning over their sick cow. They looked up when they heard me come through the barn door.

"Hey, J.W.," Joseph said as I walked into the barn. "What you doing here? Have you finished all your chores already?"

"Sure have," I replied, "and I talked my papa into coming over here so I could catch some catfish for dinner."

"Your pa must be in a pretty good mood if he let you come over in the middle of the morning," Joseph's father replied.

"He must have sold that load of watermelons I saw him hauling the other day."

"No, sir, that's not the reason," I replied. "Joseph, can we go to the lake and fish for a spell?"

"May I, Pa?" Joseph asked

"Well, only for about an hour, Joseph," his pa replied. "We've still got a lot of work to do before dinner."

"Thanks, Pa," Joseph replied, and I followed him out behind the barn where he and his pa kept their fishing poles. Joseph didn't have any brothers, only three sisters. I guess that's why we had become such good friends.

I was just busting to tell Joseph about my papa's decision, but I decided to wait until we had gotten settled at our favorite fishing spot. Then I told him.

Joseph didn't look very surprised to hear Papa's plans.

"So that's why your pa is in such a good mood," Joseph said with a smile. "He knows his farming days are over."

"I guess you're right," I replied. "He told Grandpa yesterday. When I heard him come in late last night, he was whistling."

"I'm sure going to miss you, J.W.," Joseph said as he pulled up his line with a slippery catfish hanging on it.

"I don't want you to miss me, Joseph," I said angrily. "I want you to help me think of some way to make my papa change his mind."

"I'm afraid I'm not very good at understanding why adults do the things they do," Joseph said. "I know I'm a year older than you and I can do a few things better than you, but I think you need to talk to an adult about this. Why don't you call our teacher? I bet he could help."

"You mean Mr. Haggard?" I said with a laugh. "I can't imagine talking to him about anything—especially this. He hates me anyway. When all the kids came back to Bunker Hill after being expelled from the school near Lufkin, he was fit to be tied."

"Well, what about Don's teacher?" Joseph suggested.

My older brother was in high school and his teacher, Miss Alsouth, was kind of nice. She didn't frown all the time like Mr. Haggard, and she looked like she would be a nice teacher if I ever got to high school.

"Do you know where Miss Alsouth lives?" I asked.

"She lives with her parents on their farm," Joseph said. "Why don't you give her a call and see what she says."

We did have a telephone in our farm house, but I had never used it. It was for the adults to use, primarily in emergencies. All of us kids had pretended to talk on it when Ma wasn't looking, and Don had even listened to someone on our party line talking. But none of us had actually made a call on it.

"You know how to use the telephone, Joseph?" I asked.

"Sure," Joseph replied. "That's because I'm the oldest child in my family."

"Could we call Don's teacher from here?" I asked.

"Sure," Joseph said, "but we need to catch some more catfish. My hour isn't quite up. I thought you wanted to catch some fish, too."

"Well, I did, but I also wanted to come up with an idea to keep Pa here."

"Maybe Miss Alsouth will think of something," Joseph replied. "Just let me catch one more fish, then we can go into the house and call Don's teacher for advice."

That sounded good to me. I knew that Joseph would come up with an idea.

 Three

Before Joseph's hour was up, we both had caught five catfish. Since there were six people in my family, he said I could take two of his home for my ma to fry for dinner.

"Thanks, Joseph," I said. "That's sure nice of you."

"Your pa might like more than one," Joseph insisted. "I know how tasty your ma can make them. Does she have some kind of special recipe?"

"Not that I know of," I replied. "She's just a real good cook."

"Are you about ready to make that phone call?" Joseph asked.

"Sure am!" I replied.

I started running back to Joseph's house with him following me as fast as he could, carrying a bucket of catfish.

When we got to his house, his ma was still washing clothes, so we went up to her and told her that we had caught enough fish for my whole family, thanks to Joseph's generosity.

"You boys are amazing," Mrs. Glenn said with admiration. "Your pa will be mighty happy, J.W."

"I'm sure he will be," I said. "He loves catfish even better than I do."

I looked at Joseph to see if he was ready to go inside to try to call Miss Alsouth, but he wasn't moving.

"Ma," he finally said. "I need to ask you about something very important. J.W.'s got a problem and he came over to talk with me about it. He needed some advice."

"What's your problem, J.W.?" Mrs. Glenn asked.

I was reluctant to tell Joseph's ma about my family's problems. In fact I didn't know that Joseph was going to say anything to her, but she always seemed interested in my family, so I decided to go ahead and let her know why I was so troubled.

"My papa has decided he wants to give up the farm and go back to Marshall to work," I explained. "This has been a bad year, as you know, and Papa just doesn't think he's cut out to be a farmer."

"That's a shame, J.W." Mrs. Glenn said with concern. "But how did you think Joseph could be of help?"

"I thought he might be able to come up with an idea to help me change Papa's mind. After all, he is older than me," I told her.

"But the only idea I had was to call his teacher. Teachers are smart people and usually like to help kids," Joseph said.

"But I didn't want to talk to my teacher because he hates me, so I decided to call Don's teacher, Miss Alsouth. Don says she is real nice. Joseph thinks she might have an idea."

"Oh, I know Miss Alsouth," Mrs. Glenn said. "She does seem nice and very pretty, too."

"So Joseph suggested that I try to talk to her using your telephone. He says he thinks she lives with her parents near our school," I explained. "May I?"

"Have you ever used a telephone before, J.W.?" Mrs. Glenn asked.

"No, ma'am. None of the children are allowed to. But Joseph says he will help me."

"Oh, I reckon it's okay," Mrs. Glenn said as she put more dirty clothes in the wash kettle. "But don't get your hopes up, youngun. She's a nice teacher, but she's not a magician. That's what you need. You need someone to turn pieces of corn into gold, like the magician we saw at the fair last summer."

"Yes, ma'am, I remember, but at least I can try."

Joseph and I went into his house through the kitchen and into the dining room where a big, round table sat. The brown-stained telephone hung on the wall in the corner. We had one just like it. It had been installed at the same time that all of my neighbors got their phones. There were about eighteen phones on our line. Our signal was two long rings and two short rings.

Joseph contacted the operator and asked her to ring the home of Miss Alsouth's parents. Her family was one of those on our party line. He held the phone until somebody answered, and then he began talking through the speaker while he held the other piece to his ear.

"Is this where Miss Alsouth lives?" Joseph asked. "I'm a student in the school where she teaches. I need to talk to her."

Joseph smiled one of his big grins.

"She's home, J.W.," he said.

"Hello, Miss Alsouth," Joseph said when she came to the phone. "This is Joseph Glenn. I'm a friend of J.W.Gilclay. We're both students at the Farmers' Institute. J.W. needs to talk to you."

Joseph was tall enough to speak directly into the mouthpiece of the phone, but I needed some help. I pulled up a dining room chair and stood on it.

23

"Hello, Miss Alsouth," I said loudly.

It was hard to believe that she could actually hear me in her home, which was miles and miles away.

"My brother, Don, is in your class. Remember Don?"

I didn't wait for a response. I just kept charging ahead.

"He says that you are a nice teacher. That's why I thought I would call you to let you know that my family is leaving before school starts. We're going back to Marshall."

"I'm sorry to hear that, J.W.," Miss Alsouth said. "Tell Don I will miss him."

"I sure will, Miss Alsouth," I replied, "but that wasn't exactly why I called. I don't want to go back to Marshall and neither does Don. We both want to be farmers. But our papa just doesn't think he is cut out to be a farmer, so he has decided to quit. I thought you might have some ideas about how Don and I might convince him to stay."

"I wish I could help you, J.W., but it sounds as if your father has thought about this decision carefully and is just trying to do what is best for his family."

"I know that times are very hard for farmers," I said. "But I just want him to try one more year. We all like living on a farm, even though we have to work very hard."

"I know," Miss Alsouth said. "I grew up on a farm, too. But I decided that I wanted to be a teacher rather than a farmer's wife. And that's what I did. In Marshall, your father may find the kind of job that's just right for him. He'll be happier and so will you and your family. Maybe you'll find something you like better than working on a farm. Like I did."

"I don't see how we could be happier," I inserted. "That's why I'm trying to get him to change his mind."

"I understand, J.W., but you need to try to understand why

your father has made this decision. He wants to find a better way to take care of his family because he loves you very much. Just remember that."

I knew that Miss Alsouth was right, but it didn't make the idea of moving easy to swallow.

"I've got to go now," Miss Alsouth said. "Tell Don to write me and let me know how you all are doing when you get to Marshall."

"I sure will, Miss Alsouth," I said. "Thank you for taking time to talk to me."

I frowned at Joseph as I hung up the phone.

"Your ma was right, Joseph," I said. "Miss Alsouth is no magician."

Four

I walked home as fast as I could with my bucket of catfish and put it on the table in the kitchen where Ma was fixing dinner.

"Well, you did catch a mess of catfish, J.W.," Ma said with a smile. "Your papa will be very happy. Could you just help me clean them so I can fry them for dinner?"

"Sure, Ma," I said. "Where is everybody?"

"The boys are helping your papa paint the barn so it will look good to anyone who might want to buy the farm. Baby Juanita is in the bedroom playing with her cornhusk dolls. How were Joseph and his family today?"

"They're all fine," I replied. "They've decided to stick it out for another year. I wish I could talk Papa into doing the same."

"Your papa has made up his mind, J.W.," Ma said. "He's a stubborn man. You know that. But don't forget we've been here for seven hard years."

"Yes, ma'am, but I sure do wish I could think of something to cause him to reconsider. That's what I went to talk to Joseph about."

"You shouldn't have been talking with Joseph and his family about our personal business," Ma said with a frown.

"I'm sorry, Ma, but I did. Joseph is my best friend and I thought he might have an idea."

"Well, did he?"

"The only idea he had was for me to talk to my teacher, Mr. Haggard. You know how much my teacher hates me, so I called Don's teacher, Miss Alsouth."

"Oh, no!" Ma exclaimed. "You called Don's teacher? What did she have to say?"

"Well, she didn't have long to talk. But she said the reason she was a teacher was because she didn't want to be a farmer's wife and that I should understand that Papa needs to find the best way to support his family. Or something like that. I don't remember her exact words."

"That's what I think, too, J.W.," Ma said as she grabbed my hand and squeezed it. "Your papa has tried being a farmer, and he has not been as good at it as your grandpa. He needs to find something else before he gets too old."

"But what about my dream to become a farmer?" I said. Tears were beginning to burn in my eyes, but I tried not to wipe them away. "That's been my dream ever since we moved here. That's why I like it here so much."

"You can still follow your dream, J.W. It might be on a farm and it might not. When the time is right, I'm sure God will show you how to make your dream come true. Right now, it's your papa that I'm concerned about. Let's all help him."

"How can I do that?"

"Well, the first way is to help me finish cleaning this fish."

Catfish was mighty good, but mighty hard to clean. Ma showed me how to do it the way her ma and pa had taught her, and the fish were sizzling in the skillet in no time.

At noon, Ma had prepared another meal for us and we

were all sitting around the table enjoying it. I decided to make one last effort to get Papa to reconsider.

"How was Grandpa?" I asked.

"Oh, he was fine," Papa replied.

"Was he a bit surprised to hear your plans?"

"Not really. I had told him I was thinking about it before. He knew we were having a hard time."

"J.W., why don't you just let it be?" Don said. "Papa has made up his mind. We're going to Marshall."

"But what about our plans?" I shouted. "We'll never get to become farmers now! I thought you wanted to be one just as much as I did."

"I did, J.W., but I know that Papa has done the best that he could. I'll just have to wait to have a farm of my own. And so will you."

"I didn't know that you boys wanted to be farmers," Papa said in a surprised voice.

"That's because you never asked us," I said. "Don and I talk about it all the time with Grandpa. He said he thought we'd be good ones just like him someday."

"You told Grandpa that you wanted to be farmers?" Pa said. "Why didn't you tell me?"

"Because you never listen!" I shouted. "You are always thinking about your problems and your bills."

"J.W., you are being mighty disrespectful to your papa," Ma said. "Apologize."

"I won't apologize," I said. "What I said is true!"

The catfish was churning in my stomach as I got up from the table and ran out the back door toward the lake. I didn't want the other kids to see the tears that were now flowing freely.

I had really made a mess of things. I was trying to get Papa to reconsider his plans and all I did was get him and Ma angry with me. I decided to go for a swim to cool off.

I took off my clothes and dove into the lake. The water was warm from the midday sun, and I soon felt relaxed. I swam around for about half an hour.

As I was about to get out, I looked up and saw my papa coming toward the lake. He didn't have a switch in his hand as he used to when I was smaller. But he still looked mighty angry.

I thought about hiding behind some bushes near the edge of the lake, but decided that was what a little boy would do. I decided to face Papa like a man.

"J.W.!" Papa shouted. "Are you in the lake?"

"Sure am, Papa," I said. "Why don't you come in for a swim, too? It feels great."

"Come out, J.W. We need to talk."

I walked slowly out of the lake and put on my underwear that I had placed on a log with my other clothes.

"J.W., you were mighty disrespectful back there and ought to be punished."

"I know, Papa. I've cooled off now. I was just trying to get you to change your mind."

"Well, it didn't work, J.W., because I know what's best for my family. That's why we're moving to Marshall tomorrow."

"Tomorrow?" I said in disbelief.

"Yes, tomorrow. Grandpa helped me find a place to live there and last night I went over to pick up the keys. He also found a man to run the farm until he sells it."

"So that's why you went to see Grandpa?"

"I was going to tell everybody at dinner. Then you started

asking about my trip to Grandpa's and ended up being disrespectful."

"I'm sorry, Papa," I said. "I just love this farm. After all, I've been here since I was six. It's the only home I know. I sure wish Don and I were old enough to take it over."

"But you're not, J.W." Papa said firmly. "So I expect you to help me load up Grandpa's car tomorrow for our trip to Marshall."

"Grandpa's driving us in his car?"

"He sure is," Pa said. "Our new house is near the sawmill where I will be working. I think you'll like it. It's not too far from Caddo Lake. We'll have more time to go fishing and talking. Just like you said, J.W., I've been too busy on this farm. A man needs more time to be with his children and to listen to their ideas. How about it?"

I could tell Papa was excited about the move to Marshall. His frown had been replaced with a big smile.

"Sounds good to me, Papa," I said with a lot of sadness in my heart. I hoped it would go away soon.

 Five

The next morning I was awakened by the laughter of a man with a loud, high voice. I knew it was Grandpa. He was teasing my little sister again. Baby Juanita still believed Grandpa when he told her that there were wildcats nearby each time a dog made a strange sound like a coyote.

Don and Cliff were already downstairs, probably eating breakfast. They had let Sammy and me sleep late since this was moving day and there were not as many chores to take care of.

"Wake up, Sammy," I told my baby brother. "We better get to the kitchen before Don and Cliff eat all the biscuits."

When I said biscuits, my baby brother started moving fast and got out of bed before I did.

"Good morning, Sammy," Ma said. "I bet you're hungry. Where's J.W.?"

"Here I am, Ma," I replied politely. All of my anger from the previous day had been spent. I accepted the fact that we were moving. I didn't like it, but I accepted it.

"I saved some biscuits and sausage for you," Ma said. "I knew you two would be up soon."

"Good morning, boys," Grandpa said with a big smile on his bearded face. "Ready for the trip to Marshall?"

"Sure, Grandpa," I said. "As ready as I'll ever be."

The night before we had packed all of our belongings in wooden crates. We didn't have much to pack, so it didn't take long. The crates had been taken out on the back porch.

Sitting next to Grandpa was a strange man who I had never seen before.

"Boys," Grandpa said. "I'd like you to meet Mister Clark. He is going to be running the farm for me until I can find a buyer. He says that you can come fish in the lake any time your papa can bring you out."

"Thanks, Mr. Clark," I said. "That's mighty nice of you."

"I understand there's lots of catfish in the lakes around here. Is that right, boys?" Mr. Clark asked.

"There sure is," Don replied. "We had a mess that J.W. caught yesterday for dinner."

Papa came into the kitchen from the backyard where he had been loading up Grandpa's car. He was already sweating.

"Need any help, Conway?" Grandpa asked Papa.

"No, sir," Papa replied. "I think we're ready to take off."

Just as Papa said that, our telephone rang two longs and two shorts. He answered the telephone and said it was for me.

"It's Joseph," he said. "Do you know how to talk on this dang thing?"

"Sure," I replied. "Joseph taught me."

I didn't say any more, although I saw a slight smile on Ma's face as I picked up the receiver to speak. Then I remembered that I needed to stand in a chair and grabbed one from the table to use.

"Hello, Joseph," I said, "this is J.W. We're just about to leave."

"My ma told me," Joseph said. "She heard about it when she was at Bunker Hill getting some sugar to make jelly."

"Are you going to come visit?" I asked.

"I'll try," Joseph said. "I'll sure try. I have a cousin who lives in Marshall. I'll call and let him know you're moving there."

"That's nice of you, Joseph," I said.

I looked at Pa and he pointed to the car outside, indicating that it was time to hang up.

"Goodbye, Joseph," I said. "It's time for us to leave. I'll write as soon as I get there."

I went outside and saw that the other members of my family were already in Grandpa's big black Maxwell. There was room for all the children in back and Papa and Ma in front. Grandpa was driving. Our belongings had been tied to the top with ropes.

"Come on in, J.W.," Cliff yelled. "What took you so long?"

"I was just talking to Joseph on the telephone," I explained.

"Pa let you use the phone?" Don asked in a surprised voice. "You're the first kid in our family to do that!"

"It was no big deal," I told Don. "I got to use it when I was at Joseph's house this week."

But that was as far as I went. Ma knew but I didn't want to reveal my call to Miss Alsouth to anyone else. I wasn't sure how Pa or Don might react to what I had done.

"Everybody in now?" Grandpa asked. Seeing that we all were, he started the engine and drove out on the highway heading toward Marshall.

We all waved goodbye to Mr. Clark.

I looked through the back window at the only home I had ever known. Mr. Clark was already inspecting our newly painted barn. Within seconds, all I could see was the windmill that stood next to our house near Ma's zinnia garden.

Grandpa's car created big clouds of dust on the dirt road. Soon it was difficult to even see the windmill.

I could feel tears welling up in my eyes, but I knew I better stop them fast before somebody saw. I wiped them off quickly with my right hand. As soon as I did, I heard Cliff say, "Crybaby. Crybaby."

"So what!" I said firmly. "Don't you ever feel like crying?"

"Not me," Cliff said. "Only girls cry. Crybaby! Crybaby!"

"Stop it, boys," Papa said as he turned around to see what was going on. "We've still got a long way to go."

We had stopped along the way to eat a picnic that Ma had prepared. After driving almost three hours, we finally reached Marshall. It was early afternoon, but some of the kids had been lulled to sleep by the motion of the car. I was one of them.

"Hey, wake up kids," I heard my papa say excitedly. "Here's your new home."

I opened my eyes and looked out the side window which was quite dirty by now. What I saw was mighty disappointing. Our new home was a tiny shack compared to our farm house. There was no fence or porch or flower garden. If the lake was nearby, it sure wasn't almost in our backyard like at the farm. It was worse than I had even imagined it might be.

Grandpa helped us unload and then told us that he had told Grandma he would be home by suppertime.

"Let me know if I can be of any more help, Conway," Grandpa said before leaving.

"Thanks, Pa," Papa said as he walked Grandpa to his car. "I sure will."

Ma fixed a big supper of black-eyed peas and cornbread that she had prepared on her stove at the farm before leaving.

She served it on the painted wooden table furnished in our new rented home, but her cooking just didn't taste as good to me as it usually did.

After supper, I asked Ma to help me make up my bed so I could go to sleep. It had been an exhausting day and she understood that we were tired, especially me.

Before getting into bed, I found my school tablet with the big Indian chief on it and started drawing a picture of our farm. I drew the barn and the hog pen and the windmill and the lake and Ma's zinnia garden and I titled it, "My Home, 1913-1920."

Then I crawled under the quilt that Ma had put on my bed, praying that the following day would be a better day. It had to be.

SIX

My first week in Marshall went very slowly. I didn't know anybody and school hadn't started yet. I spent most of the day looking for a job to help my family make ends meet.

Papa had gone back to the sawmill and Ma was fixing meals for one of our new neighbors who had just had a baby. Sammy and Baby Juanita were helping Ma. Don and Cliff were sharing an afternoon paper route.

I finally found a job passing out flyers for the Strand, Marshall's newest picture show. I had to go from door to door, passing out colored papers about coming attractions. Mr. Granger, the manager, said that if I did a good job delivering the flyers, he would let me sell tickets someday or maybe play the player piano near the front of the theater. And I would get more money!

On the back of the flyer was an ad about the Samuel Goldwyn Company, one of the newer movie studios in Hollywood. It listed some of their new productions and said they still needed people to be players in their movies. The ad encouraged people to write to them and to send a photograph if they were interested in being in Goldwyn movies.

I had a few of the flyers left over after I had finished the route for Mr. Granger. I put them in my back pocket to share with my family when I got home.

"Did you get your job done?" Ma asked when I went into the kitchen to see what she was cooking for supper.

"Sure did," I replied, "but I had a few flyers left over so I just brought them home with me." I pulled them out of my pocket. "Would you like one?" I asked.

"Sure," Ma said as she put more flour on the pie crust for the dessert she was preparing. "Anything good coming to the Strand?" she asked.

"Looks like new movies with Charlie Chaplin and Mary Pickford are opening this week," I replied.

"Anything with Lillian Gish? She's one of my favorites."

"Yes, her new movie is going to be at the Strand. It's called *Broken Blossoms*."

Just about that time, Don and Cliff came in from doing their afternoon paper route. They were sweaty and hot from the August sun.

"What you got there?" Don asked when he saw the piece of colored paper that I was showing Ma.

"It's just an announcement for the new picture show in Marshall," I replied. "I thought I told you I got a job with them passing out flyers."

"Oh, yeah," Don said. "I just forgot."

"Anybody want to go for a swim?" Cliff asked.

"That sounds good to me," I said.

"Me, too," Don agreed. "Is it okay, Ma?"

"Sure," Ma said. "Just be back by suppertime."

We ran down to the lake near our new home and scooted

out of our clothes as fast as we could. We left them on a log the way we always did at the farm.

The water was warm but refreshing, and we swam until the sun began to set.

"It's time to go home for supper," Don said.

We all came out of the water naked as jaybirds and went straight to the log to put our clothes on as fast as we could.

"I thought we put our clothes on this log," I said to my two brothers. "I'm sure we did."

"Maybe it was the one next to it," Don said in his calm, mature voice that was getting deeper by the day.

But when we looked there, we found nothing.

"Some rascal has stolen our clothes!" Cliff yelled. "Wait 'til I get my hands on him!"

"This has never happened to us before, Don," I said to my older brother. "What do we do now?"

"Why don't you go back to the house to get dressed and bring us some clothes?" Don answered. "Let Ma know that our clothes were stolen."

Cliff thought that was a great idea.

Since I was the least physically developed of the four Gilclay brothers—except for Sammy—and the fastest runner, I agreed to do what Don asked. He and Cliff hid behind some bushes near the lake to wait for my return.

By now it was dark and I was able to get to my new home without anybody seeing me.

"What happened?" Ma asked as I walked naked into the kitchen. My younger brother and sister giggled when they saw me. I quickly grabbed a dish towel and wrapped it around my waist.

I told Ma what happened and that Don and Cliff were

waiting for me near the lake. She helped me find some clean clothes for them and for myself.

"Is Papa home yet?" I asked.

"No," Ma said. "I'm sure he will be home soon. Hurry and get these clothes to your brothers before he does. I know he will be plenty upset."

I rushed through the dark to where my brothers were shivering near a tree and gave them their clothes.

"Was Ma mad?" Don asked.

"More surprised than mad," I replied. "Papa wasn't home yet, so he doesn't know."

By the time we got home, Papa had returned from work. Ma had told him what happened and when he saw us he started laughing. I'd never heard him laugh so hard before.

"That same thing happened to me when I was a boy," Papa said, slapping Don on the back. "I never found my clothes, and I never found out who did it so I could give him a bloody nose."

"Well, I don't think it's funny at all," Ma said as she put leftover fried chicken and mashed potatoes on the table for supper. "You're all going to have to work even harder to pay for new clothes to replace the ones stolen by those bullies."

"Oh, we can do that pretty fast now that we all have jobs," I reminded Ma.

"I didn't know that you had gotten a job, J.W.," Papa said. "What are you doing?"

"I'm passing out flyers for the new picture show on Washington Street," I said proudly. "They pay me two bits for every hundred flyers I distribute. If I do a good job, I may get to sell tickets and I'll get a raise."

"That sounds like a mighty good job," Papa said. "You'll

soon be making about as much as I'm making at the sawmill. I'm only making $1.25 a day. That movie business must be pretty good."

"Would you like to see one of the flyers?" I asked Papa.

"Sure," Papa said as Ma poured him more coffee.

"A new Charlie Chaplin movie is coming next week," Ma said. "I know you like the Little Tramp."

"Yeah, I sure do," Papa said, "but I like westerns even better. Any William S. Hart movies coming?"

"Not this week," I replied, "but I'll let you know when one is."

Papa read aloud all the movies that were coming to the Strand and then he turned the flyer over. He read the ad from the new Samuel Goldwyn Company.

"Want to become a movie star, Ma?" Papa asked. "Looks like the Samuel Goldwyn Company is looking for more players to be in their movies."

"Oh, sure," Ma teased. "Mary Pickford is getting thousands of dollars a week to act like a little girl in all her movies. I think I could do that."

Ma giggled as she began to wash the supper dishes with the help of Baby Juanita. I didn't know Ma and Papa knew so much about movies. I guess since motion pictures were new, people talked about them a lot. I had heard Ma mention the high salaries that some of the stars were making. Her mother had read about it in the newspaper.

"Be serious," Papa said. "I think you're as pretty as Mary Pickford. Why don't we send them your picture? The ad says that's all we have to do."

"Well, what about your picture, Conway?" Ma retorted. "To me you are as handsome as Douglas Fairbanks."

"You never told me that," Papa said.

"Why don't you just send in both of your pictures?" Don said. "Then the people in Hollywood can decide which one of you would be best."

"That's a good idea," Papa said. "That's a dang good idea. Thanks for bringing the flyer home, J.W. Your Ma and Papa will soon be rich movie stars."

I could not believe that my parents were really serious, so I played along with their little fantasy as I went to bed.

"Good night, Miss Pickford and Mr. Fairbanks," I said as I left the shabby kitchen of our rented house and went to my bedroom that I shared with my three brothers. "Tell the butler to awaken me when it's time for breakfast."

Then I went to sleep wondering who had stolen our clothes.

Seven

By the time I woke up, Papa had already left for work. Ma was in the kitchen rewriting the letter they had composed together to send to the Goldwyn Company along with their pictures. Don and Cliff had gotten up early to look for the bully who had taken our clothes. The younger kids were playing in the corner with their Christmas toys.

"Good morning, J.W.," Ma said. "Would you like to hear our letter?"

Ma put down her pencil and began reading without a reply to her question. She had used the lined tablet on which she always wrote letters to relatives and notes to my teachers.

"Dear Mr. Goldwyn," she began. "We saw your ad on the flyer that my son, J.W., was distributing for the Strand Theater. It said that you still needed players for your new movie company. I think my husband, Conway, is handsome enough to be in your movies, and he thinks I am as pretty as Mary Pickford. That's why we are sending you our pictures. We also have four handsome boys and a beautiful five-year-old daughter we call Baby Juanita. We all play musical instruments and sing at church socials. Maybe we could all be players in your movies. Sincerely, Conway and Noonie Gilclay."

"That sounds fine to me, Ma, but why did you have to say anything about the kids?" I asked, a bit irritated. "You know I want to be a farmer, and so does Don."

"I know," Ma said, "but I just thought Mr. Goldwyn should know that we had a family. My mother reads about Mary Pickford and Douglas Fairbanks in the paper all the time. She told me that they recently got divorced and married each other. She was pretty upset about it, but she said it would have been worse if they had had any kids, so the article must not have mentioned any. If Mr. Goldwyn hires our whole family, he will get a real bargain."

"I understand, Ma. Do you want me to mail the letter when I go to pick up my flyers for the day at the Strand? I go right by the post office."

"Oh, that sure would be nice," Ma replied. "Let me see if I can find some stamps to put on it. This picture is pretty heavy."

After a breakfast of pancakes and sausage, I said goodbye to Ma and told her that I would mail the letter at the post office on my way to the Strand. I had never mailed a letter in a post office before, so I asked the man behind the counter how.

"My ma asked me to mail a letter for her," I explained. "Do I give it to you?"

"Yes, young man," the postmaster said with a smile. "I'll take it, but the next time you come in, you can just stick it in that slot over there that says 'mail.' All outgoing mail goes through that slot."

I gave the letter to the postmaster and he read out loud where it was going.

43

"So your ma has written a letter to Hollywood, California?" he said.

"Yeah," I replied, "she thinks we can all become movie stars, but I really want to be a farmer like my Grandpa. How long will it take the letter to arrive?"

"Just a few days," he said. "Isn't that amazing? You can send a letter all the way to California in less than a week. That's because the Texas and Pacific Railroad will pick it up and take it there this afternoon."

"That is pretty amazing," I agreed. "It's also amazing that you could just stick a letter through that slot in the wall and it ends up being delivered to a person miles and miles away. Thanks for you help."

"You're mighty welcome," the postmaster said as I left the post office.

When I got to the Strand Theater, Mr. Granger looked quite upset.

"J.W.!" he shouted excitedly. "I'm so glad you finally got here. The piano player man is sick and I need you to fill in for him today. I'll show you how it is done. It's really quite easy once you get the knack of it."

Mr. Granger had told me that some day I might get to sell tickets and maybe even play the player piano that was used to accompany the silent movies, but I had no idea it would be during my first week at the Strand!

"I don't know how to play a piano, Mr. Granger," I said. I was sure that my lack of experience would put an end to the matter.

"Neither does Billy. He just selects piano rolls from our collection and plays them at the appropriate times. There is a cue sheet that the movie producers provide to let you know when you need to change the type of music. I've already picked out the piano rolls for today's movies."

Mr. Granger was not the type of man to take no for an answer. I was soon sitting at the piano, reviewing the rolls of music, and learning how to pump the pedals that made it go.

"The first movie is a Pearl White serial," Mr. Granger said as he reviewed the cue sheet with me. "I've selected one exciting number that should last the entire movie. The next one is a comedy with Charlie Chaplin, and I've selected one lively number that should last the entire movie since it's short. To change from one roll to the other, you take it out and put in a new one after rewinding the old one. You can even use the drum and whistle if you want. Chaplin's movies usually have people kicking each other or falling down. The last movie is the main feature starring Lillian Gish. It's over an hour. I've selected several rolls of melancholy songs that you can play over and over again because her movies are always sad. Any questions?"

Actually I had a lot, but I didn't want Mr. Granger to think I couldn't do the job. After all, this might mean that I would get that raise that he said would come if I did well distributing flyers.

Just about 1:00 P.M., kids and adults started flowing into the Strand and took their seats behind me. I felt as if they were all staring at me until the lights went out and the projector started. I began the player piano just as the titles for the serial appeared on the screen. The music that Mr. Granger had selected for the *Perils of Pauline* fit it very well. The final scene showed Pearl White in another cliff-hanger ending.

I put in the roll that he had selected for *Sunnyside*, the Chaplin movie. The film was a short two-reeler in which the actor portrayed the Little Tramp. The music Mr. Granger had selected was just perfect. About half way through the Chaplin film there was a fight, so I hit the drums and, when it was over, blew the whistle that Mr. Granger had pointed out to me. Everyone was cheering at the end when the Little Tramp triumphed again.

Finally, the titles for *Broken Blossoms* appeared on the screen and I began the music that had been selected. Lillian Gish played a little girl who was abused by her father and found refuge in the shop of a Chinese merchant. By the time the movie was over, everyone was in tears, including myself, but they still applauded as the lights came back on. I turned around and smiled. I felt as if they were applauding me as well as the movies they had just seen. After all, I had provided the music and a few sound effects, but my legs were really tired!

"Mr. Granger was right," I said to myself. "This isn't so hard."

Before I could go tell him how I had done, another crowd was coming in and the title for the Pearl White serial was up on the screen again.

I did one more show. Then Mr. Granger said I could go home for supper. The family was already eating when I arrived.

"Hey, J.W." Ma said. "You're a bit late. I hope the boys saved some food for you. Be sure to wash up before you sit down."

I could hardly wait to tell the family what I had been doing all day. They would never believe me.

"Did you get all the flyers delivered?" Don asked.

"Well, not exactly," I said, beaming. "Today they asked me to substitute for the piano player. He had a bad cold. I got to play it for two shows and then Mr. Granger told me to go home and get some supper. He's filling in for me right now. I've got to go back as soon as I finish supper."

"You don't know how to play the piano," Cliff said. "Why did he ask you?"

I explained how the player piano worked and how I had used the rolls that Mr. Granger had selected after he had reviewed the cue sheets.

"I even played the drum during the Charlie Chaplin comedy," I said proudly.

Everyone seemed quite amazed with my success playing the player piano, including me.

"Well, I've got to get back now," I said as I finished a bowl of blackberry cobbler. "Mr. Granger is expecting me to come back to do the piano for the last show."

That night as I helped Mr. Granger close up the Strand, several people from the last show came up to me and said what a good job I had done filling in for Billy.

As I walked home that evening, I began to think about how much I had enjoyed performing in front of the movie audience. Maybe I did have some talents that even I knew nothing about, like Miss Alsouth had said, and maybe being a farmer was just one of them. I fell asleep exhausted but very, very happy.

#

It was almost time for school to start again. The summer had gone so fast. I had been working at the Strand for nearly a month. The regular piano player had returned, so I was back delivering flyers. I didn't mind. I'd had my moment of glory, and I must admit I liked it.

My duties had expanded, though. I was now helping sell tickets when Mr. Granger was busy. I also helped paint signs to advertise coming attractions. The manager had seen me drawing a picture in my Big Chief tablet and thought I was a pretty good artist. I was soon drawing pictures of cowboys and cowgirls to advertise the western movies that were coming. So I was now making almost a dollar a week just like Mr. Granger said I would.

Papa was still working at the sawmill and Ma was selling pies and cobblers to the neighbors. They had not yet heard from the Samuel Goldwyn Company about their letter. Don and Cliff were still sharing their paper route and trying to find the bully who had taken our clothes. Sammy and Baby Juanita were having a quiet summer meeting new friends and getting ready to go to their new elementary school in Marshall.

When I got home from work that night, Ma was wearing a very big grin.

"What you so happy about?" I asked her. "Did you find a pot of gold?"

"Something like that," Ma said, "but I'd rather wait until your papa gets home to talk about it."

When Papa arrived, Ma almost knocked him down as he walked through the door.

"The letter came!" Ma shouted.

"What letter?" asked Papa.

"The one from the Samuel Goldwyn Company," Ma said excitedly. "It's signed by Mr. Sawyer, one of Mr. Goldwyn's assistants. He says he can use us both but doesn't say anything about the rest of the family. All we have to do is get to California."

"Well, that could be pretty expensive," Papa said. "I don't want to ask my pa for any more money."

"I could ask my mama," Ma said. "After my father's death, she seems to be doing fine in her big old house. I think he must have left her pretty well off."

Ma's father had been a farmer and an amateur musician. He used to ride all over East Texas on his black stallion, participating in singing contests. He died before I was born. According to Ma, he had a deep bass voice that won every contest he had ever entered. He brought the prize money home to Grandma who hid it in her mattress safe.

"How much money are we talking about?" Papa asked. "We need to check with the railroad depot on the fare to Hollywood for two adults and five children. Don, why don't you and the boys run down to the train depot and find out for us?"

Our new home was about a mile from the train depot, so we ran down and back in less than an hour. Sammy was the only one who had any trouble keeping up, so I gave him a Piggy Back ride most of the way home.

Don reported his findings to Papa. The rest of us were huffing and puffing from the run.

"That's a lot of money," Papa said. "Noonie, are you sure you want to ask your Ma for it?"

"She knows we have been having a hard time making ends meet," Ma replied. "I'll explain that this will help us make a fresh start and that we may be able to pay her back if we're successful there."

"With all of us working in the movies, we may be able to do that sooner than we think," Papa said. "Some of the movies have little kids in them as young as Juanita."

"Why don't I give her a call and see what she says?" Ma replied.

Our new telephone had been installed just a few weeks before, but the only people who had used it were Ma and Papa when they talked to Grandpa.

Ma went to our new phone and talked to the operator about the call she wanted to make. Soon my other Grandma was on the line and they were talking. The telephone still seemed like a miracle to me. I thought it was the greatest invention ever.

Ma explained to Grandma why we needed money for the train fare and what we planned to do when we got to Hollywood. Grandma had seen a Charlie Chaplin movie one time so she knew what Ma was talking about. She had told Ma that she had never laughed so hard in all her life. Ma reminded her that Charlie Chaplin lived in Hollywood and made his movies there.

"But we will be working for the Samuel Goldwyn Company," Ma said. "We sent them our picture and they wrote us a letter telling us to come on out and be some of their players."

Ma had not actually read the letter to us, so I didn't know exactly what it said, but I'd never seen her and Papa so excited about anything in all my life. Ma hung up the phone with a big smile on her face.

"Well," Papa asked "what did your mother say?"

"She said she would wire the money to us tomorrow," Ma said.

Everyone in the room cheered. Even me. It looked like we were all going to Hollywood to be players at the Goldwyn Company—whatever that meant.

Ma and Papa made becoming rich movie stars sound easy.

My mind was reeling with the thought of another move. I had just accepted the fact that I would no longer be a farm boy and had become a city slicker by moving to Marshall. Just as I was getting used to being there and had a job and was making friends, Papa and Ma now wanted to move again to a place that none of us had ever even been to—Hollywood!

Personally, I was sure they were making a big mistake, but I pretended I was just as excited as everyone else in my family.

"We'll leave just as soon as we can make travel arrangements and quit our jobs," Papa said. "Why don't you talk to the manager at the Strand about our plans tomorrow, J.W., and I'll do the same at my job."

I sure hated having to tell Mr. Granger that I had to give up my job because we were moving. Maybe he had actually been to Hollywood and could tell me what it was like there. It would be nice for someone in the family to know what we were really getting ourselves into. Some of the movies that I had seen made being a player look really dangerous. I decided to ask Mr. Granger about it the following day.

Nine

The next morning when I arrived at the Strand, Mr. Granger was changing the signs that announced the current movie.

"Good morning, J.W.," Mr. Granger said. "Aren't you a bit early?"

"Yes, sir," I replied, "but my papa wanted me to tell you as soon as I could so you could find another boy to help you."

"Another boy?"

"Yes, sir," I replied. "My papa and my ma have decided that they want to be players in the movies, so they wrote to the Samuel Goldwyn Company. Yesterday they got a letter saying that they would put the whole family to work if we could just get to California. I think it's a stupid idea, myself! But everybody's excited about going, including Baby Juanita. Have you been there?"

"Yes, J.W., I have. Before I became the manager of the Strand, I went out to Hollywood to meet some of the people who produce movies and met a few of the stars. Lon Chaney was one of them. I know you're a fan of his. The movie business is booming and there are all kinds of jobs there. The climate is great and you can have fresh oranges from your own tree."

"Maybe I could be a farmer there and grow oranges," I replied. "I've always wanted to be a farmer like my Grandpa."

"Sure, J.W.," Mr. Granger said, "you could probably be anything you want there. California is called the 'land of opportunity.' I'm sure going to miss you."

"But isn't it kind of dangerous being a player?" I asked. "I sure don't want Ma to be tied to a railroad track the way Pearl White is sometimes."

"Oh, they do a lot of things to fool the audience by using doubles and sometimes stunt men," Mr. Granger explained. "I've never heard of anyone getting hurt making a movie. Maybe it has happened, but I've never read about it."

"That's good to hear," I replied. "Being a farmer was dangerous enough for me. I almost got gored by one of my Grandpa's bulls one time. Thanks for answering my questions. I feel better now."

When I got home that night, I told Papa and Ma that I had quit my job.

"I quit mine, too," Papa said. "Looks like there's no turning back now."

"And the train fare came today," Ma said. "Looks like we're all set."

That evening we called our relatives and friends and told them our plans.

"I just can't believe it," Joseph said when I finally got to talk to him. Papa had to talk to his mother and father first. "Will you all be in the movies?"

"Could be," I said. "Samuel Goldwyn is one of the newer companies. That's why they need more people for their movies. I have no idea what Papa and Ma are going to do as players, but I'll write you soon."

"Be sure to draw me a picture, too."

"Sure will," I replied. "Ma has packed my tablet and pencil in her suitcase. We're all ready to go."

Grandpa drove us to the station in his Maxwell. Grandma had fixed us some food to eat on the train during our long trip from Marshall to Hollywood. Before we knew it, the Texas and Pacific locomotive had pulled up beside us.

We all gave hugs and kisses to Grandma and Grandpa and told them we would write them as soon as we got to Hollywood. We had never been on such a long trip before. We wanted them to know that we had arrived safely.

This was our first train trip, so we were pretty excited. Papa and Ma let me and my two older brothers walk down to the snack bar on the train to get soda pops for everyone to drink with the noon meal. When we returned, Sammy and Baby Juanita were fast asleep. The motion of the train was very relaxing.

Ma had packed all of our belongings in suitcases that she had borrowed from her mother. I asked her for my tablet and pencil so I could draw a picture of the inside of the train, but the ride was too bumpy to do too much drawing.

In fact, there wasn't much to do on the train trip except eat, sleep, and go to the toilet. I had never been to the toilet on a train before, but it was just like our outhouse at the farm except the train had tissue paper on a roll rather than an old Sears catalog. Personally, I missed having the old catalog to browse through.

"When are we going to get there?" Baby Juanita kept asking. She didn't understand that the trip was going to take several days.

As we moved toward the West Coast, I kept thinking about what Mr. Granger had said. He had called California the land of opportunity.

I had never heard that word before…opportunity. I guess he meant that in California, I could be a farmer or I could be a movie star or I could be an artist or I could be whatever I wanted. I had never felt like that in Texas. There I just wanted to be a farmer like Grandpa.

"Ma," I said on the last night of our train trip, "Mr. Granger said that California is a land of many opportunities for a young man like me. What do you think he meant?"

"He probably meant that you'll have more choices there than back in Marshall, and so will your papa. But when we arrive tomorrow we'll be able to see what he meant, J.W. Go to sleep."

I was having a hard time falling asleep. I was finally getting excited about moving to Hollywood. I was anxious to see what my new home state was really like and to find out about all those opportunities Mr. Granger was talking about.

 Ten

"Wake up, J.W.," Ma said. "We're finally here."

I looked out the train window and Ma was right. From my seat, I could see the golden river that rushed along the train track and the narrow gravel streets that ran right up to the foothills. It looked like some kind of bushes came next and then lots and lots of hills. The sky was the bluest blue I had ever seen.

"Look, Ma!" I shouted. "Those are the tallest mountains I've ever seen. Joseph will never believe me when I write him about this."

"You'll have to draw him a picture, too," Ma said.

"That's a good idea," I replied. "I think I'll start on it now."

As we approached the Hollywood train depot, I drew Joseph a picture of what I saw. The ride was a bit bumpy, but I had finished drawing it in pencil by the time the train stopped. I could fill in the details later after we got settled in our new home.

When the train stopped, we all got off. There was a strange smell in the air.

"What's that smell?" I asked.

"It's poppy seeds," Don replied. "The porters threw them on the track as we approached. They even let Cliff and me help them. They said it was to make the air smell fresh and sweet."

"I didn't see you do that," I replied. "I guess I was still sleeping."

"That's right, sleepy head," Cliff teased. "They said they did it each time they approached Hollywood. The porters said it was a tradition."

There were taxis waiting at the train depot to drive people who did not have anyone to pick them up. Papa had already told us that we were going to stay in a boarding house when we first arrived.

"We're from Texas," Papa told the taxi driver. "We're going to be working for the Goldwyn Company. The letter we have says the studio is in Culver City. Could you drive us to a boarding house that's close by?"

"Sure thing," the driver said. "What part of Texas are you all from? I have some relatives there, myself."

"We're from Marshall," Papa said. "It's in East Texas. We have lots of pretty scenery there, but nothing like this."

"You're right about that," the driver said, "and the weather is mild here most of the time. That's one of the major reasons why some of the movie people decided to come here."

The whole family got into the taxi and started driving down Hollywood Boulevard, which was also just a gravel road. There were tall palm trees along the side and rose bushes growing in front of many of the buildings.

"This looks like the Garden of Eden," Ma said excitedly as she pointed to the roses. Those flowers were certainly more beautiful than the zinnias that she had planted near our farm house in Texas.

"There's a boarding house up there on the right," the driver said, "but I don't think they will take movie people. Some of the old-time residents in Hollywood resent the newcomers and won't rent to them. They feel like they have been invaded by a bunch of wacky strangers."

"Mr. Granger didn't say anything about that," I whispered to Ma. "Maybe that's because he just came out for a visit."

We finally found a boarding house on Washington Boulevard that didn't say "No Actors" and Papa went in to see if they had room for us while we waited.

Papa had a big smile on his face when he came out.

"They've got two rooms left, Noonie," Papa said. "One for you and me and Juanita and the other for the boys."

The driver unloaded our suitcases from the taxi and we walked into our new home.

"Welcome to Hollywood!" the woman who owned the house said with a warm smile. "Just follow me upstairs, and I'll show you to your rooms."

Papa followed the woman up the stairs, and Ma followed him with Baby Juanita holding her hand. Next came Don, Cliff, Sammy, and me. The second floor had several bedrooms and a bath. The house reminded me of Grandpa's big house in Texas.

"You'll share the bath with my other boarders," the woman said. "And we all eat together two times a day for breakfast and dinner. You're on your own for lunch."

I had never heard anyone talk about lunch before. In Texas we had dinner at noon and supper in the evening. I'd have to ask Ma what the lady meant after we got settled.

"We also provide linens, and you'll get clean ones every week," the woman concluded. "Any questions?"

"Not now," Papa said, "but where do you stay in case we do?"

"My room is on the first floor near the kitchen," she responded. "Just knock if the door is closed."

It was almost dinnertime and my stomach was beginning to growl. It had been a long time since breakfast, which had been just a donut and milk on the train.

"Anybody hungry?" Papa asked. "The lady said dinner would be served in the dining room and it's almost noon."

We all agreed that we needed food and followed Papa downstairs to the dining room. But it was empty.

"I thought the lady said that dinner was served in the dining room, Noonie," Papa said with a puzzled look on his face.

"She did, Conway, but she didn't say what time. Why don't we knock on her door and ask."

Papa looked a bit angry as he knocked on the door to get the lady's attention.

"We're all mighty hungry," he told her. "We thought you said dinner would be served in the dining room."

"That's right," the woman said smiling, "but in California, dinner is what we call our evening meal. I serve it to my boarders at 6:00 P.M. We call our noon meal lunch, and you're on your own for that. Some of the boarders keep fruit and other fixings to make lunch in their rooms, and you're welcome to do the same."

"Well, in Texas we call our evening meal supper," Papa said. "I think you can see why we're a bit confused."

"I sure do," the boarding lady said with a laugh. "I'd recommend that you walk down the street to Joe's hot dog stand for lunch. I bet you boys like hot dogs."

Papa smiled as the lady was talking. None of us had ever eaten a hot dog.

"I appreciate the suggestion," Papa said, "but what exactly is a hot dog? We've never eaten one before. Is it like a hot tamale? We've eaten them before. We have lots of hot tamale stands in Marshall."

"Not really," the lady said, still smiling. "It's more like a sausage in a bun with mustard and relish on it."

When the lady said sausage, my eyes lit up.

"We all love sausage, Papa!" I shouted. I was about ready to eat a mud pie, I was so hungry. "I bet we will all love hot dogs."

"Maybe," Papa said cautiously. "Where is this stand you're talking about?"

"It's just right down the street across from Goldwyn Pictures," she said. "Tell him Mrs. Malloy recommended it to you."

We all walked down the street from Mrs. Malloy's boarding house. The sun was bright and we could see a tall set behind the gray, stucco studio walls. There was a huge iron gate guarding the entrance and a sign saying Goldwyn Pictures Corporation of New York. The gold-plated sign sparkled like it was on fire.

"Look, Papa!" I shouted. "That's where you and Ma are going to be working."

"You're right, J.W.," Papa replied. "I didn't realize how close it was to the boarding house. The taxi driver had just said it was on the same street. I thought it could be miles away like in Texas."

In Texas, it did seem like everything was a long way off, but here everything was kind of all together.

"Hey, kids," Ma said. "There's a junior high school. I bet that's where J.W. will be going to school. We'll have to ask Mrs. Malloy where the high school and elementary schools are. Maybe we can even find an apartment near the Goldwyn Company."

When we got to the hog dog stand, Papa ordered one for each of us with all the trimmings and sodas, too. We then took them to a nearby park and had our first family meal in Hollywood. Papa even said the blessing the way he always did at home.

Papa was thankful for many things. He had traveled safely with his family many miles to a state where they had different names for meals and different foods to eat.

But were things really going to be different here? Would Papa be able to support his family the way he wanted to? Would he and Ma really be good players in the movies? And what kind of new opportunities was I really going to have here?

My mind was full of so many questions as I sat at the picnic table eating my first hot dog that I barely heard Papa ask me what I thought of it.

"It's okay," I replied.

"Only okay?" Papa asked. "I think it's real good! I'm glad Mrs .Malloy recommended this place, and it's only just across the street from where Ma and I are going to be working. When we become rich movie stars, we'll come over here for lunch a lot, Ma."

Ma was just as excited as Papa and she agreed with his opinion of our first hot dogs.

As I washed mine down with orange soda pop, my hunger had been satisfied, but a piece of country sausage in a biscuit would have tasted much, much better. But I decided just to be thankful that I was full again. And I decided to avoid hot dogs in the future, if I could.

Eleven

After we finished our hot dogs, Papa wanted to go across the street to see Mr. Goldwyn's assistant, who had sent him and Ma the letter about coming out to Hollywood to be players.

"We might as well go over and let him know we're here, Noonie," Papa said.

We followed Papa across Washington Boulevard up to the entrance to Goldwyn Pictures. There was a security guard near the big metal front gate. He didn't look very friendly.

"We're from Texas," Papa told the guard, "and we'd like to see Mr. Goldwyn's assistant. Is Mr. Sawyer in?"

"I don't think so," the guard said. "I think he's helping with a production that's shooting today on location out of the studio. He should be back tomorrow. What did you say your name was?"

Papa told the guard his name and asked what time would be best to come back.

"Thanks for your help," Papa told the guard. "I'll see you tomorrow at nine sharp."

We walked back to Mrs. Malloy's boarding house. As we passed a few people, they curled up their noses and made a strange noise that sounded like my grandpa calling his pigs.

"What's going on?" I asked Papa.

"I think they're trying to tell us we smell bad," he replied. "You know, it has been about two weeks since we all had a good bath."

"It sure has," Ma added," and your Pa and I need to look our best when we go back to see Mr. Sawyer. We better get back to the boarding house and use Mrs. Malloy's tub."

Papa reported to Mrs. Malloy on our trip to the hot dog stand and told her that we had gone across the street to Goldwyn Pictures.

"Are you going to work there?" Mrs. Malloy asked.

"Yes," Papa replied. "Noonie and I sent our picture to Mr. Goldwyn's assistant. We then got a letter from him saying to come on out and we could be players in Mr. Goldwyn's movies."

"What a coincidence," Mrs. Malloy said. "Another boarder works there also. Her name is Sally Clark. You will meet her at dinner tonight."

"That sounds great," Ma said, "but right now we need to go upstairs and use your tub. We were on the train for several days, so it's been quite a while since we all had baths."

"Well, there should be plenty of hot water," Mrs. Malloy said, "since no one has recently taken a bath. I'll get you each a clean towel from the laundry room."

After Mrs. Malloy had given us clean towels, Ma unpacked our suitcases. One was filled with our clothes and the other with hers and Papa's. Then she started getting us all bathed, beginning with Baby Juanita. All of the boys were old enough to bathe themselves, but Mama had to help us fill the tub with water. We usually took our baths in tin tubs either outdoors or in a corner of the kitchen. This was the first time for us to take a bath in a porcelain tub in a real bathroom. The younger children were pretty excited and wanted to play awhile by splashing the water and pretending they were swimming in the lake near our farm.

While Ma was unpacking our suitcase, I asked her to give me my tablet and pencil, and I worked some more on that picture I had drawn for Joseph. I really liked to draw. When I earned some money, I planned on getting me a real sketch pad and colored pencils like I had seen in the store in Marshall. When I had taken my bath, I decided to write him a note describing our first day in Hollywood to go with my picture.

"Dear Joseph," I wrote. "Well, we finally made it! We spent several days on the train and were pretty stinky when we arrived. I just took my first bath in a real tub. We're staying in a boarding house until we can afford to have our own place. Sammy and I are sharing the same bed, just as we did in Texas. I haven't seen Charlie Chaplin yet, but when I do I'll write again. I did see the biggest mountain I've ever seen and drew you a picture of it. Your friend, J.W."

After I finished the note, I decided to take a nap. I was still pretty exhausted from our long train trip. The next thing I knew, I heard Ma's voice.

"Wake up, boys," Ma said. "It's supper...I mean... dinnertime."

We followed Papa and Ma downstairs to eat dinner. It was 6:00 P.M. and all of the other boarders had gathered around the big long table in the dining room.

"Sit wherever you like," Mrs. Malloy said. "All the others are already here. I did get out a highchair for Baby Juanita."

Ma helped Juanita get into the high chair and the rest of us found places in between the other boarders. Don sat next to a pretty blonde with pale blue eyes. I sat across from the plate of fried chicken. I had never been so hungry in all my life.

After we sat down, Mrs. Malloy crossed herself and said the blessing.

"Bless us, oh Lord, and these Thy gifts that we are about to receive from Thy bounty through Christ, our Lord. In the name of the Father, the Son, and the Holy Spirit."

That was the blessing Ma's mother always said when we visited her. Mrs. Malloy must be Catholic like Ma and Grandma.

When she had finished, we began passing around the food, family-style. I felt like I was back in Grandma's house. Mrs. Malloy had prepared fried chicken and mashed potatoes and gravy and cole slaw. She had also made lots of biscuits and several cobblers for dessert. One of them looked like peach, one of my favorite kinds. We washed the food down with cool lemonade. It was the best meal I had eaten in a very long time.

"Sally," Mrs. Malloy said, "our new boarders are also going to be working at the Goldwyn studio. How about that?"

The beautiful blonde responded to Mrs. Malloy's comment. "Are you going to be players, too?" Sally asked.

"We hope so," Papa replied. "We saw an ad about Goldwyn Pictures on the back of a flyer J.W. was delivering for a picture show in Marshall. It said they still needed players in their movies. Ma wrote a letter and sent a picture just like they asked for. We then got a letter from Mr. Sawyer, Mr. Goldwyn's assistant."

"I have it in my purse," Ma inserted.

"Oh, yes, I know Mr. Sawyer," Sally said.

"The letter said that Noonie and I photographed well and

we could be used as players if we could just get out to Hollywood," Papa continued.

"We borrowed the money from my mama," Ma said honestly. "That's how we got here. We're going to see Mr. Sawyer tomorrow to let him know that we're here."

"That sounds almost like my story," said Sally, who looked as if she was a few years older than Don. "I saw that same ad and wrote to them just like you did. My mother and daddy were set against me coming out here 'cause I didn't know a living soul. But Mrs. Malloy just took me under her wing and I've been doing fine. Right, Mrs. Malloy? I know I'm going to be a star in no time."

"What movies have you been in?" Ma asked.

"Well, I've been in several Mabel Normand movies as an extra," Sally replied. "She is one of Goldwyn Pictures' biggest stars. I was also in a Lon Chaney film at Paramount. Mr. Chaney will begin his first movie for Goldwyn tomorrow."

"What's an extra?" Papa asked.

"An extra is a person who is on the movie screen but is not one of the principal characters," replied Sally. "In *The Miracle Man*, I was in the church scene where Lon Chaney pretends to change from a cripple to a well man. It was an incredible scene and he did it without the camera even stopping."

"I remember seeing that movie at the Strand," I said. "I'm a Lon Chaney fan, Miss Clark. I can't believe I'm eating supper with someone who was in one of his movies. That was really a great one!"

"Being an extra doesn't pay as well as being a star," Sally continued, "but that's how a lot of stars were discovered. Gloria Swanson is a good example. She started out as an extra in Mack Sennett comedies, and look at her now."

"You're right," Papa said. "More power to you, Miss Clark. I'm glad we're going to be working for the same studio."

The next morning, we all got up early and ate breakfast with the other boarders. Miss Clark did not eat breakfast. She was already at Goldwyn Pictures acting an extra in the new Lon Chaney movie.

At breakfast, Mrs. Malloy mentioned that public schools began the following week. Papa asked Don to go to the high school to get registration papers so we could all start on time. Education was very important to Papa, and he didn't want us to miss getting started on time just because we had moved to a new state. He'd had to quit school to help support his family and didn't even have a high school education. He didn't want that to happen to his children.

After Papa and Ma left for their appointment with Mr. Goldwyn's assistant, Cliff and I walked a few blocks to the high school that he and Don would be attending. Mrs. Malloy agreed to take care of Sammy and Baby Juanita for the day.

Although I was not anxious to have another hot dog, we told Ma and Papa that we would meet them at Joe's stand for lunch. We arrived around noon and looked inside, but they were not there yet. Then we looked outside on the street and saw Papa and Ma coming toward the stand. Papa was really upset! His face was red and he was yelling at Ma. We went outside to see what the problem was.

"What happened?" I asked. "What did Mr. Sawyer say?"

"He said we were too old to be players," Papa replied. "That picture Ma sent with our letter was our wedding picture. Mr. Sawyer saw that and didn't even read Ma's letter about us having five children. That picture was taken when we were in our late teens, not much older than Don."

"Do we have to go back to Texas?" Don asked. "I did get the school forms you asked for, but I didn't start filling them out."

"No, we can stay here, Don," Papa replied. "They can use us as extras. They need older people for extras. That's what Sally has been doing ever since she came here."

"That sounds good," I said. "What about us kids?"

"I didn't ask Mr. Sawyer about you kids," Papa replied, "but I bet they can use you, too. I bet Sally will know. But you all will be in school soon. What did you find out about school, Don?"

Don explained that we could all start the following week. He and Cliff would be in high school, I would be in junior high, and Sammy and Juanita would be in elementary school. He said all the schools were close to each other and we could walk there.

"Sounds great," Ma commented. "Anybody hungry?"

"We sure are!" my brothers and I shouted.

"Since it doesn't look like we are going to be movie stars as fast as I thought, why don't we go to the store and get some things for a picnic?" Papa suggested. "Those hot dogs yesterday were pretty expensive."

We went in a small grocery store on Washington Boulevard and bought a loaf of bread and some peanut butter. Papa used his pocket knife to spread it on the slices. We sat in the park and ate our lunch quietly. We got one soda and passed it from person to person. I could tell Papa and Ma were still mighty disappointed about their meeting with Mr. Sawyer.

"Did Mr. Sawyer have any other ideas about jobs for our family?" I asked.

"He did apologize for the mistake," Papa replied, "and said he could use me in his publicity department if I were interested. I told him yes."

"What's a publicity department?" I asked.

69

"If I understood Mr. Sawyer correctly," Papa said, "I would be doing things to let people know about new movies from Goldwyn Pictures and helping with openings."

"He called them premieres, I believe," Ma inserted. "That's a new one on me."

"On me, too," Papa replied. "But he said that's when the stars come out and the people can see them in person."

"Even Lon Chaney?" I asked.

"Even Lon Chaney," Papa replied. "As a matter of fact, Mr. Sawyer said I could help with the premiere of the new movie that Lon Chaney started today."

"Wow," I said. "California really is the land of opportunity for Papa."

We all ate our peanut butter sandwiches in the park. They tasted much better than the hot dogs that we had bought the day before.

When I got home, I added a "p.s." to my letter to Joseph and finished my drawing.

Mrs. Malloy walked by my room and saw my drawing. She asked me if I'd like to have some crayons to color it with. Her children were now all adults, but she still had some of their old crayons and colored pencils in a tin box.

I had never had so many crayons before and I felt very special as I sat by the window and looked out at the setting sun. I made the sky a bright orange just like what I was seeing and then I colored the mountains brown and the sagebrush green.

At the bottom of the picture I wrote, "Land of Opportunity."

When I showed it to Ma, she had said it was the best picture I had ever drawn. I folded it neatly and put it in an envelope on which I wrote Joseph's address in Texas.

In my "p.s.," I told Joseph what Ma and Papa would be doing at Goldwyn Pictures now that we were really here. I also told him the whole family might be extras in some future Goldwyn movie and that I would be sure to let him know what it was. I also told him about our first hot dog and bath in a tub and that we might attend the opening of Lon Chaney's next movie.

"You better get to bed, J.W." Ma said as she came into the bedroom that I shared with my three brothers. "We need to get you and the other kids registered for school tomorrow. School begins Monday bright and early."

"Okay, Ma," I said as I sealed the letter and gave it to her. "Could you ask Mrs. Malloy where to mail letters in Hollywood? I want to get this one to Joseph as soon as I can."

As I said my prayers, I thanked God for getting us to Hollywood safely and having a job for Papa here and that Mr. Goldwyn would think he was doing a good job so he wouldn't get fired. I'd sure hate to see my family out begging for food the way I had seen some do back in Marshall because they were having trouble finding a job after the war. I also prayed that I would soon be back in Texas learning how to be a farmer like Grandpa. So far I had not seen anything here that seemed better than that. Not one thing.

Twelve

The next Monday morning, Ma got us all ready for school. We had been at the boarding house for almost a week. Don and Cliff were off to Hollywood High. Juanita and Sammy were off to Blessed Sacrament, a Catholic elementary school near the boarding house, and I was off to Hollywood Junior High to be in seventh grade. Mrs. Malloy's children had gone to Blessed Sacrament, and she highly recommended it to Ma. There was no school bus, so on the first day, we all took the red street car that traveled down Washington Boulevard from early morning until late evening.

Papa had left early along with Sally Clark for his job in the publicity department at Goldwyn Pictures. Mr. Goldwyn had approved an advance on Papa's salary because of the confusion about the letter Mr. Sawyer had sent. Sally was still working as an extra in the new Lon Chaney movie and had to be at work the same time as Papa.

Ma said goodbye when she and the younger kids reached Blessed Sacrament.

"Have a good day, boys," Ma yelled. "I want to hear all about it after work."

Ma was helping Mrs. Malloy with the cooking at the boarding house until they needed an older woman as an extra. Don and Cliff and I rode for another half mile and then we got off and walked to our schools. It was hard to believe we had actually walked five miles to and from school in Texas.

When I got to my school, Don gave me a pat on the back and said, "See you after school. Don't let any bullies push you around just because big brother's not there."

"You don't think I can take care of myself, huh?" I asked. "I'm almost as big as you and Cliff. I'm not worried about bullies. I just hope there aren't any teachers like Mr. Haggard! That's what I'm worried about."

"They'll all be as sweet as Miss Alsouth," Don teased, "and they'll all love my little brother's baby face!"

"I sure hope so," I said with a big grin as I waved goodbye to my two older brothers.

Ma had asked me if I wanted her to go with me to school on the first day, and I told her absolutely not. No self-respecting thirteen-year-old boy wanted his Ma going with him to school, even if it were the first day. It would be too embarrassing!

When I had gone to the school to register with my brothers, they gave me my schedule because I was registering so late. My first-period class was physical education, and I was supposed to report to the gym.

It was a beautiful, sunny California day so we all went outside. First we did exercises, and then the boys played softball and the girls played something where they were dodging a big rubber ball. I had never seen that game before, but softball I knew well from my school days in Texas. The school provided all the equipment. We had a real softball to play with instead of a homemade one.

The next class was history, which was one of my favorite subjects, and the next was English, which was not. Then it was time for lunch. The morning had really gone fast.

I picked up my tray of food and went to a table where four other boys were eating. One of them looked like Joseph with freckles and red hair. I thought he might be a good person to talk to.

"My name is J.W. Gilclay," I said as I sat down next to him. "I'm new to the school. How long have you been here?"

"We're all new to the school, stupid!" the tallest boy at the table said. "All of us were in elementary school last year. Where were you?"

"I was in Texas," I replied. "My school was a lot smaller than this one. We only had two teachers."

"Are you a cowboy?" the tall boy asked sarcastically.

"No," I replied. "I was a farmer."

"A farmer," the boy said with a laugh. "Did you ever milk any cows?"

"I sure did," I said proudly.

"Then I bet you know a lot about tits, farmer boy," he said, glancing over at one of the girls with large breasts.

"Don't pay any attention to Chester," the boy with red hair advised. "He's always showing off."

"What do you mean, Mr. Clown Face?" the tall boy said. "You're the showoff with your red hair."

"Don't talk to my friend like that," I said.

I had just met the boy, but he was sure friendlier than Chester, and I needed a friend in Hollywood.

I was definitely not the biggest kid in the seventh grade, but I wasn't going to let this bully push me and my new friend around—especially not on the first day of school.

My friend and I got up from the table, and so did Chester. He came toward me swinging his fists and I pushed him back. He lost his balance and fell on his behind. That really made him mad. Soon he was up and swinging harder than before, and I grabbed him around the middle.

"Fight! Fight!" one of the other boys at the table yelled.

Chester and I were rolling around on the linoleum floor of the cafeteria when the teacher on duty made us stop. He sent us to the principal's office near the front of the school.

We sat there for about a half an hour staring at each other and cooling off before the principal called us in.

"What happened, gentlemen?" the principal asked.

We both told our stories. Naturally they were quite different.

"I want you to shake hands, gentlemen, and tell each other you are sorry," the principal said. "I don't want this to happen again."

"I'm not sorry," I told the principal. "If he hits me again, I'll hit him back."

Chester said nothing.

"Well, if that's the way you both feel," the principal said," I want you to sit outside my office the rest of the day and think about your unacceptable behavior."

Chester and I sat outside the principal's office for the rest of the day. My new friend came by and waved on his way to his last class of the day.

When the bell rang for the end of the day, I gave Chester the toughest look I was able to put on my "baby face" and walked out of the principal's office.

The freckled-faced boy who was my new friend was waiting for me.

"My name is Bill, Bill Meadows," he said as he put out his hand to shake. "Sorry you had to run into Chester on your first day at school. What happened in the principal's office?"

I told him the whole story and what I had said to the principal.

"Incredible," Bill said. "You had lots of guts. I would probably have said I was sorry even if I didn't mean it."

"My papa has always taught me to never lie," I said, "and I never have."

"What do you think your Pa will think about what you did today?" Bill asked.

"That's a good question," I told my new friend. "I'll let you know tomorrow at lunch."

When I got to Mrs. Malloy's boarding house, Ma was already there with Juanita and Sammy. Don and Cliff were not home yet.

"How was your day?" Ma asked.

"Can we talk in private?" I replied. I didn't want the younger children to hear what had happened. Ma gave the kids some toys to play with and we went into my bedroom to talk. I told her the whole story.

"That's a terrible way to get started in a new school, J.W. Your papa and I want you to like it here. But I think you did the right thing. Let's wait until after dinner to talk with Papa about what happened. I'd prefer we not talk about it with the other boarders."

After dinner, Ma suggested to Papa that we take a walk down the street and asked me to come along. Ma told Papa the story of my first day at Hollywood Junior High while I listened. I thought Papa would be proud of what I had done, but I wasn't sure. On the other hand, he might want to send me back to Texas, which was exactly what I wanted.

"I've run into a lot of bullies in my life, J.W.," Papa said "and I've learned one thing. You have to stand up to them. You cannot let them push you around. If you do, they will just come back and bother you some more. I'm sorry you missed some of you first day of school, but I think you did the right thing. I'm mighty proud of you."

Papa then stopped walking. He looked me straight in the eye and gave me a strong handshake and a pat on the back.

I felt like giving him a big fat hug, but I had never seen him do that with Grandpa, so I didn't.

"Thanks, Papa," I said. "I knew you would understand."

We continued our walk until we were outside of Goldwyn Pictures. A sign was being placed on the bulletin board near the front gate. We walked across the street to read it.

The sign said:

> 100 extras needed for a crowd scene in a new comedy on Saturday from 8:00-6:00. Children and adults of all ages needed. Pay will be four bits per person plus lunch.
>
> DO NOT WEAR SHOES!

"Hey, Papa," I said, "that sounds like a great way for me and the other kids to earn some money."

"I agree. Me and Noonie could do it, too," Papa replied. "Let's go back and tell them about it."

When we returned to the boarding house, the rest of the family was worried about us.

"I was about to come out looking for you," Don said. "I didn't know you were going to be gone for so long."

"We were just walking and talking and kind of lost track

of the time," Ma replied. "J.W. had something he wanted to tell Papa about his first day at school."

"Did you get beat up?" Cliff asked.

"Nope," I replied, "but I did have a fight with the tallest boy in school and we were taken to the principal's office."

"Wow!" Cliff said. "I thought you were Mr. Goody-Goody. No wonder you didn't want us to know."

"We had a pretty boring day," Don said, "so Cliff is happy to know that someone had some excitement."

"Yeah, Don is right," Cliff said, "but I did have lunch with the cutest girl I've ever met. She came from Texas, too, and her parents are movie people."

"Talking about movies," Papa said, "how would you all like to earn some dough as extras on Saturday? They'll also give us lunch. We saw them putting up a sign about it when we passed the Goldwyn studios."

"That sounds great to me," Cliff said. "I need some money. I've decided to invite my girlfriend out for a soda next week after school. What do we do?"

"Well, I'm not really sure," Papa said, "except you don't wear shoes."

"No shoes?" Cliff asked. "That sounds fine with me. I hate wearing shoes anyway."

We all agreed that being extras at Goldwyn Pictures on Saturday was a good way for the entire family to earn some extra money and have some fun, too.

Maybe Papa's crazy idea to come to Hollywood was really going to work out. Maybe we would all be discovered and become rich movie stars quicker than I thought. But was that what God wanted me to do with my life? I thought He wanted me to be a farmer like Grandpa.

That night I had a dream about being a movie star. In my dream, I was at the premiere of my first movie. At the end of the movie, all the lights went on and the audience rose and applauded me for my incredible performance.

"Bravo! Bravo!" the audience shouted in my dream. "Bravo!"

When I woke up, my body was covered with cold sweat and I was screaming, "No! No!"

I woke up my three brothers. Cliff and Don thought I was anxious about being an extra and they started teasing me about it. I couldn't tell them that I was having a nightmare, so I just said, "Sure. That was it."

I was anxious to get away from this wacky family and be on my own as soon as I could. I still wanted to be a farmer like Grandpa. What was wrong with that? Grandpa had been happy, and he would help me get started when I returned to Texas. He had said he would. My mind was racing with all that had happened since we arrived in Hollywood. It took me a long time to get back to sleep that night. A very long time.

Thirteen

The rest of my first week at school was quiet compared to the first day. On Tuesday, I saw Chester in the cafeteria, but he did not bother me. I had lunch with Bill and some of his friends from elementary school. They were friendly and had lots of questions about Texas.

I told them Papa was working for Goldwyn Pictures and that they needed lots of extras on Saturday for a crowd scene in a new comedy.

"My whole family is going," I told them.

"That sounds like a fun way to earn some money," replied Bill. "I'll ask my mom if I can come, too."

On Friday, Bill said his Mom had told him it was okay and he would meet me at the Goldwyn studios on Saturday morning.

At dinner, Papa told all of the boarding house residents about the need for extras the next day.

"I think I'll come, too," said Sally Clark. "I can always use the extra money."

After dinner, Papa and Ma talked with Mrs. Malloy about apartments in the area. My parents planned to move into one at the end of September, now that Papa had a steady job working in the publicity department at Goldwyn Pictures. Mrs. Malloy had a friend who owned an apartment building on Norton Avenue, not too far from the studio. It was owned by the mother of an aspiring movie star. Mrs. Malloy called her friend and told her she had a family interested in renting an apartment. Her friend said Papa and Ma could come right over.

When Papa and Ma returned, they were quite excited.

"We found a perfect apartment," Ma said. "It has three bedrooms, a living room, dining room, and one bath."

"You boys won't have to sleep in the same bedroom anymore," Papa said.

"And there is a park nearby with a small lake for fishing."

"And it has a rose garden in between the two walks at the entrance to the apartment," Ma added.

"I used some of my advance from Mr. Goldwyn to put down a deposit," Papa said. "Looks like we will be able to move in on the first of October."

"I didn't think you would be able to find something so soon, Papa," I said. "Things are really happening fast here." *Too fast for me*, I thought.

The next morning we all got up early and ate breakfast in the dining room with the other boarders. Sally Clark was there, too.

"What are you going to be doing at the studio today?" Mrs. Malloy asked as she passed around a plate of biscuits.

"To be perfectly honest, I'm not sure," Papa answered. "We've never been extras before."

"It's easy. All you do is listen to the director," Sally explained. "He uses a megaphone and sometimes stands up high on a platform so everyone can hear what he says."

"But why can't you wear shoes?" Mrs. Malloy asked. "J.W. said that you are not supposed to wear shoes."

"It probably has something to do with the plot of the story," Sally inserted. "Maybe we are all shipwrecked on a desert island off the coast of Arabia and will be looking for the sheik to come rescue us on his yacht."

"That sounds like the plot for a Theda Bara movie, Sally," Mrs. Malloy responded. "I thought this was supposed to be a Goldwyn Pictures comedy."

"You're right, Mrs. Malloy," Ma said. "I think Sally was just getting a little carried away. We'll tell you all about it when we get home."

Don reminded us that it was time to leave. Since we were running a little late, we all got on the streetcar and rode down to the studio. Ma and Sally decided to wear their shoes and would take them off later. Papa and all the kids went barefoot.

It was a good thing that we took the streetcar, because there was already a crowd inside the studio entrance when we arrived, even though it looked like it would soon be raining. We were among the last ten people to be allowed in. Bill had already gone inside and was waiting for us. We had agreed earlier not to wait for each other because my family was often late. When Bill saw me, he came over to say hello. I introduced him to my family. Then I heard a loud voice asking for our attention. A man was standing up on a high platform so he could talk directly to all of us.

"Good morning," he said. "I am David Thomas. I am an assistant director here. I will be directing this sequence today. How many of you have been extras before?"

Practically everyone raised their hands except my family and Bill.

"That's good. I like to have experienced people. The first thing you must do is to take off your shoes if you are wearing them."

Ma and Sally and several other women took their shoes off and placed them in their purses or tote bags.

"Now let me explain why you should not be wearing shoes," the director continued.

I moved up closer so that I could hear what the director said. I wanted to be sure that I did this right and was just a bit nervous.

"In our story, all of the shoes in the town have mysteriously disappeared. People wake up in the morning and find the shoes have disappeared from beside their beds. They think they may have been stolen by the city leaders, so they go from building to building shouting, 'Shoes! Shoes! Shoes!' We'll shoot the scene in the street outside of the studio."

I had seen them shoot movies in the street before even in my short time in Hollywood. Movie film required very bright light, and it was cheaper to use natural sunlight rather than the bright klieg lights inside the studio. Mrs. Malloy said that some of the old timers in the town did not like it because it was so disruptive. But she thought it was kind of exciting and so did many of the visitors who stayed with her.

"What do we do if it starts raining?" one man asked.

"If it's just a sprinkle, keep going, but if it's really hard, stop and find shelter," the director said. "I'll let you know by saying 'Stop.' Any other questions before we move into the street?" the director asked. "You can start with the building right in front of the studio. Then move down the street to where the cameraman is set up. But wait until I say 'Action.'"

I had a million questions, but I seemed to be the only one.

Everyone seemed to be very calm about working as extras. Sally Clark had said it would be easy.

We all walked outside of the studio and up to the building right in front without saying a word. There was one cameraman at the end of the street ready to operate a hand-cranked camera supported by tripods. We waited for the director's signal to begin.

"Action!" the director said, and we all ran up to the first building shouting, "Shoes! Shoes! Shoes!"

We then went to the second and then the third building. Then I heard the director yell through his megaphone, "Stop the action!"

We all stopped and turned to him to find out what was wrong. It had not started to rain. What had we done wrong?

"Your faces don't look as if you are really angry about your shoes disappearing," the director said. "You need to look as if your shoes are the most important piece of clothing you own. You are incredibly angry because they have been stolen! Let's get some anger on those faces! Let's start again with the first building."

We all moved back to the first building and started all over again. This time I tried to look really angry, but I wasn't sure it was because I was trying to act or because I was really angry that we were in Hollywood and that I had suggested that we try to earn some money by being extras.

"Excellent!" the director shouted. "Now go to the next building and the next and the next!"

At last it looked as if we were doing what the director wanted when we heard him shout, "Stop the action! Someone has been hurt!"

In our eagerness to do exactly what the director wanted, an older woman had been knocked over by some teenage boys.

No one in my family had done it, thank goodness. The woman had to be carried off the street by two men. She was about Mrs. Malloy's size and age. It could have been Ma!

"Let's take a ten-minute break, then start again from the beginning," the director said.

From the beginning? I thought. I had no idea that making a movie could take so much time. We spent the rest of the morning moving from one building to the next and shouting angrily about our lost shoes.

At lunch time, baloney sandwiches and chips from the commissary were brought out by the cooks and served on big tables inside the front gate. Papa said the studio was one of the few to have its own cafeteria, but it was closed on Saturday and Sunday.

"You have thirty minutes for lunch," the director said.

I looked around for Bill so we could eat together. All of the extras stood and ate sandwiches and we washed our food down with soda. I was so hungry! I could have eaten a horse, so naturally I had a second even though baloney sandwiches are definitely not my favorite food! Bill had two also.

"Well, what do you think about being an extra?" I asked.

"I like it," Bill said. "I"m having fun. How about you?"

"To be perfectly honest, I'm finding it a bit boring. I'm not sure I want to do this again."

Sally Clark saw us and waved.

"Who is that?" Bill asked. "She's beautiful."

"Oh, she's one of the boarders at the house where we're now staying," I told my friend. "I think my older brother has a crush on her. She came out here like a lot of people to become a movie star. She's been an extra in several movies including one with Lon Chaney. She is working on his newest movie at Goldwyn Pictures right now."

"I've seen a lot of people like her myself," Bill replied.

After lunch, the director told us to go back in the street again. This time we were running from building to building on the other side of the street and the cameraman had moved to a new location.

"This time," the director said, "you are pretending that you have found your shoes and are smiling. You are shouting 'Shoes! Shoes! Shoes!' with big smiles on your faces. If you brought your shoes, you can put them on now. ACTION!"

"What a weird movie," I said to Bill. "It's hard to see how this is all going to fit together. I wonder if we will be able to see ourselves in the final version?"

Just as I was contemplating our movie debut, it started to pour.

"STOP THE ACTION!" the director said as he ran for cover as well.

For the next two hours, Bill and I sat and played cards under an awning with my brothers. Sammy and Baby Juanita played with their Christmas toys. Ma always came prepared to keep the younger children busy in case of an emergency. Papa went into his office to do some work until the rain stopped.

About mid-afternoon, the director told us that we could start again. By sunset, the filming was done. "You've done a good job in spite of the bad weather," the director said. "You can all go to the cashier and collect your pay."

Papa let Bill go ahead of him in line and he collected his money first, and then Papa got the pay for the entire family. I said goodbye to Bill and told him that I would see him at school on Monday.

"Thanks for letting me know about today," Bill said. "I really enjoyed it."

"Yeah, a lot more than me," I replied.

When we got back to the boarding house, we had dinner with the other boarders and told them about our first day as extras.

"I think I know that woman who got hurt," Mrs. Malloy said. "She loves being in movies. I'll give her a call and see how she is doing after dinner."

As I ate my apple pie, I heard my family and Sally talk about what a great day it had been.

"Maybe this will be the time when somebody important sees me and decides to make me a star," Sally said dreamily.

"Maybe," Papa said as he patted Sally's shoulder in a fatherly manner. "You're certainly pretty enough."

I was just happy that the boring and almost disastrous day was over and that I had *not* been discovered! I definitely did not want to be a movie star. But in my short time in Hollywood, I had seen too many people who did and would probably do almost anything to get a chance. They made me want to throw up, including Sally Clark, even if my big brother did think that she was mighty cute. He treated her like she was a star already. Sometimes Don and Cliff could be disgusting, too. Especially about girls.

Frankly, I was ready for the next train back to Texas, but I didn't have enough money saved to buy a one-way ticket. I thought it was about time I got a job in Hollywood. Mr. Granger said there were all kinds of jobs there. But Papa wanted me and my older brothers to wait until we got our first report cards so he would know we were off to a good start in school.

Fourteen

By Halloween, our family was settled in our new apartment on Norton Drive. It was the nicest home we had ever had! Papa was doing well in his job at Goldwyn Pictures in the publicity department. He had accepted the fact that his place in Hollywood was behind the scenes. Papa had a knack for coming up with ideas for promoting movies that got people into the theaters. He came up with the ideas of giving away prizes to the first one hundred people who bought tickets for a new picture show and conducting look-alike contests for some of Goldwyn Pictures' most popular stars.

Ma's feelings about being a movie player had also changed after almost getting hurt during our day as extras in the new Goldwyn comedy. She had gotten a part-time job at a florist not far from our apartment. The florist had many Hollywood stars as customers. Ma would be driven every week to their homes and decorate entire houses with flowers.

The weekend before Halloween, Ma took me and Sammy and Juanita to help her decorate the home of Norma Shearer, an actress that Ma said would soon be a big star. We decorated her home with white roses which the florist said that Miss Shearer particularly liked.

We went from room to room in the spacious home, helping Ma take out the flowers that had been brought earlier and replacing them with fresh roses. Then we brought in a large arrangement of yellow and orange mums to put on the table in the front hallway. It took us over an hour to decorate the elegant house. I'd never seen anything so beautiful before. The maid said that Miss Shearer was at the studio making a movie, so we did not get to meet her.

In Hollywood, the stars were treated like royalty, and Ma was very excited about doing this on a weekly basis. All of her new friends, especially Mrs. Malloy, were quite curious about what Norma Shearer's house looked like.

Don and Cliff decided they needed to earn money on a more regular basis than just being movie extras. Since all of the paper routes in our neighborhood were already taken, they decided to become ushers at a movie theater within walking distance of our new apartment. I volunteered to help out when one of them was sick.

My older brothers were old enough to get driver's licenses. In California, the age limit was fourteen, but we did not yet have a car to drive and we relied on being able to walk or use the street car to any place we wanted to go. Ma left for her job with the florist in time to take Sammy and Juanita to school, and Don walked them home and took care of them until Ma returned.

Now that I had decided to return to Texas for a visit to see Grandpa and Joseph, I needed to earn some money fast, but what kind of job was right for me in Hollywood? I sure didn't want to be an extra again, and I had already worked in a movie theater in Marshall like Don and Cliff were doing. I decided to talk with Ma about it.

I suggested to Ma that we take a walk after I helped her wash the dinner dishes.

"Well, J.W., what did you want to talk about?" Ma asked.

"I need a regular job, Ma, like Don and Cliff," I blurted. "They are working as ushers and saving money for a car. I need money to travel back to Texas during Christmas vacation to see Grandpa and Joseph. I really miss them. I wish I could just go back there and stay, but don't tell Papa I said that. He wants us all to be happy here. But I'm not."

"Why don't you talk with your papa about being an office boy at Goldwyn?" Ma replied. "I know Mr. Sawyer said they need help there."

"I don't want Papa to get a job for me," I said. "I want to get one on my own, just like Don and Cliff."

"Well, I did hear from one of the girls at the florist that they are looking for office boys at Metropolitan Studios," Mama said. "That's one of the smaller companies. I've seen their building on my way to work. It's not far from Hollywood Junior High. Why don't you go by there after school tomorrow and talk to them?"

"Well, what does an office boy actually do?" I asked. "I never met an office boy when were living in Marshall."

"Your papa could probably answer that better than me," Ma said. "Why don't you talk with him?"

"No," I replied, "then he would know what I am up to. I'd rather wait until I actually have the job."

"I understand," Ma said, "but be sure to ask a few questions when you go in."

The next afternoon after school, I walked to Metropolitan

Studios. Ma was right. They had a big sign in the window that said:

OFFICE BOY NEEDED

I walked into the front office and told them that I was interested in the job.

"What's your name?" the man behind the desk asked.

"J.W. Gilclay," I replied.

"Have you ever been an office boy before?" he asked.

"No," I replied, "I've only been in Hollywood since September. My papa came here to work for Goldwyn Studios."

"Well, your major job would be taking messages around to people here at the studio," he said. "You may also be asked to do some banking for people like cashing paychecks for employees."

"I think I can handle that," I said confidently.

"How old are you, J.W.?" the man asked.

"Almost fourteen," I said proudly. "My birthday is November 30."

"Do you have any transportation?" he asked.

"Not yet," I said.

"That's okay," he said. "Until you do, you can use the studio bike to go the bank. When you get your driver's license, you can use one of the studio cars. When can you start?"

"How about tomorrow?" I said. "Am I hired?"

"You sure are," the man said. "You look like a hard-working and trustworthy young man. Don't give me any reason to change my mind."

"I sure won't," I said. "Oh, by the way, how much will I make?"

"Two bits an hour," he replied.

"That sounds terrific!" I exclaimed. "I'll see you tomorrow after school."

At the dinner table, I proudly announced that I now had a job in Hollywood, too.

"I'm the office and messenger boy at Metropolitan Studios," I explained. "I'll be working for three hours every day after school. I'll still have time to do my homework and play on the baseball team with Bill."

"Congratulations!" Papa said in a surprised voice. "Looks like the whole family is working in the movie business except Sammy and Juanita. Why didn't you tell me you were looking for a job as an office boy? We need several down at Goldwyn. How did you find out about this job?"

"One of Ma's friends at the florist told her about it," I replied. "He hired me on the spot."

"I'm proud of you, J.W.," Papa said. "I think my family is doing pretty well in Hollywood. What do you plan to do with your money? I know Don and Cliff are saving to buy a used car that they can share."

"I want to go back to Texas, Papa, to visit Grandpa and Joseph during my Christmas break," I said without looking him in the eye. "I"m still pretty homesick."

Papa didn't say a word. There was nothing but silence. I could tell he was disappointed to hear me say it, but it was true. I was still miserable in Hollywood. I couldn't lie to him. Then Don picked up the dinner conversation.

"You're right, Papa," Don said, "we are doing pretty well, but I've still never seen one movie star and have never been on a movie set except when we were being extras out on the street. I told all of my friends that I'd write them when I did, but it's never happened."

"Most of the studios don't give tours," Papa explained, "and the stars come out to meet the public only when a premiere is scheduled."

"How about taking a tour of your studio?" Cliff asked. "I've never done that."

"I'll see what I can arrange," Papa replied, "but don't count on it."

After dinner, Don and Cliff went off to their jobs as ushers and I worked on my homework in the room I shared with Sammy and Juanita. Sammy and I had bunk beds, which I had never seen before. He was also working on homework and having some trouble with his arithmetic, so I helped him with that since math was my best subject.

When Don and Cliff came home from their jobs around eleven o'clock, Don came into my room to see if I was still awake.

"What do you want?" I asked.

"Just wanted to talk with you about a great idea that Cliff and I had," Don whispered. "Meet us after the late movie tomorrow night and we'll tell you about it. Tomorrow is Friday. Okay? I don't want Ma and Papa to hear us."

"Okay," I replied, but I was very curious to know what the idea was.

My day at school was just as boring as ever. Bill and I did have fun at lunch talking about another kid who wouldn't let Chester push him around either.

"Looks like everyone is standing up to Chester now," Bill said. "And this boy is even smaller than you!"

After school, I rode the streetcar to Metropolitan Studios and reported for my first day of work at 3:00 P.M.

"Good afternoon," I said to the man who hired me. "I'm ready to start."

"Good to see you, J.W.," Mr. Burns replied. "I'll show you around the studio first, and we can deliver the mail and some of the messages that came in today."

Metropolitan was a small studio, but they had most of the same departments that you would find at a larger one. The art department looked especially interesting.

My tour of the studio took about fifteen minutes. Everyone was very friendly and welcomed me to my new job.

After we were finished, we walked back to the front office and I just sat by the window waiting for Mr. Burns to ask me to do something and thinking about what it would be like to work with the men in the art department. Through the window, I saw a cameraman and some actors. One of them was Harold Lloyd, one of my favorite comedians. They were shooting a scene for a new movie. At last, I was seeing a movie actually being made with a star I recognized. I could hardly wait to tell Don and Cliff and the rest of the family. And Joseph would have to know as well. I'd have to write him and maybe draw a picture to go along with it.

I left the studio at 6:00 P.M. and walked home for dinner. Don and Cliff were having dinner with the family before going to work at the Merck Theater. I told the whole family about seeing Harold Lloyd acting out a scene for his new movie and everyone was really impressed. I also told them about my tour of the studio and how much I liked the art department.

"Don't forget about coming to the late show," Don whispered as he left.

"Oh, sure," I said.

At eight o'clock, I told Papa and Ma that I was going to catch the last movie and walk home with Don and Cliff.

"They're showing Lon Chaney's new movie, *Treasure Island*." I told them. "Cliff and Don said it's really great. Chaney plays two roles in it."

"Have fun," Papa said. "Glad you are going to do something fun with your brothers. All work and no play makes for a dull life, or something like that."

The late show ended at midnight and I met Don and Cliff in the lobby. The theater was a big one that seated about 1,500 people. Quite different from the Strand in Marshall. In the lobby there was a large painting of Samson knocking down the temple columns.

"What is this great idea?" I asked excitedly. "I can't wait any longer."

"We're going to take a tour of Goldwyn studios," Don said. "Just follow me."

Fifteen

It was after midnight as we walked down Washington Boulevard to the Goldwyn Pictures studio. Don led the way and Cliff and I followed. No one said a word.

When we got to the block where the studio was located, Don motioned to us to follow him through a long alley that ran beside it. Large trash cans used by the different departments lined the alley. I almost ran into one as I tried to keep up with my older brothers.

When we got to the back of the studio. there was a tall, wooden fence with a big red sign that said:

No Trespassing!

"Don," I whispered, "we're going to all get caught and Papa is going to give us the licking of our lives!"

"No, we won't," Don said. "One of my friends did this at another small studio. He said that most don't even have guards in the evening. It will be fun to see where Papa works."

"Come on, J.W.," Don said. "We'll let you over the fence first."

I put my foot in Don's hand and he lifted me high enough that I was able to get to the other side.

"I made it," I whispered, but it looked like I didn't need to be quiet. Don was right. There did not appear to be anyone else around.

Don helped Cliff next and then he hopped over the wall on his own. He was definitely the strongest boy in the family. I looked forward to being just as tall and strong very soon.

"Let's try to find the publicity department," Don said. "That's where Papa works."

We began walking when we almost fell into a big pool of water. In it was floating a large ship with tall sails.

"Wow!" Cliff said. "That sure looks real. I wonder what movie that is for?"

"We can ask Papa," I replied. Then I remembered that we couldn't even let him know what we were seeing.

On the next set, we saw what looked like a sculptor's studio.

"I bet that's where they are filming the new Lon Chaney movie," I said. "Papa told me all about it. He knows I'm a real fan of Mr. Chaney. He said in this movie he plays a legless man who is a gangster. Papa said that the gangster wants to have new legs grafted onto his stumps, so he so he tries to get a surgeon to do it by being nice to his daughter. The daughter is a sculptress, and he poses for her sculpture of Satan. She thinks Chaney looks like a fallen angel. Sounds great, doesn't it?"

"I never have liked Lon Chaney movies," Don said. "I may pass that one up, too. I prefer Douglas Fairbanks. Now those are exciting movies!"

"Well, Papa said that we might all get to go the premiere of the new Chaney movie and maybe even meet him like Papa has," I replied. "This is the first movie he has made for Goldwyn Pictures. Papa said they are paying him five hundred dollars a week! What do you think about going to a real premiere?"

"Sounds great to me," Cliff replied. "I wonder what Lon Chaney really looks like. He seems different in every movie that I've seen him in."

"You're right," I replied, "but Papa said he reminded him of one of our uncles back in Texas. He said he was ordinary in looks and size. But I still want to meet him."

We walked past the set and saw a dressing room with Lon Chaney's name on it.

"See, guys!" I shouted. "This is where Mr. Chaney puts on his makeup."

The door was open so we looked inside. There was a dresser with a big mirror over it and a open makeup kit with Mr. Chaney's name on it. Over the chair was a leather harness.

"See the harness on the chair," I pointed out. "Papa told me about that. He said Mr. Chaney devised it to strap his lower legs to the back of his quads so he can walk with heavy leather stumps on his knees. Isn't that incredible!"

"That must be why they are paying him so much money," Cliff said. "I've never heard of any actor getting paid so much except for Douglas Fairbanks."

"Come on, guys," Don said impatiently. "I want to see where Papa works."

We continued to follow Don through the dark Goldwyn Pictures studio looking for Papa's office.

"There's the art department," Cliff said.

I peeked my head inside and saw some miniatures of the Lon Chaney set that we had just walked by earlier. There was also a large drawing board on which the hand-lettered title cards for a new movie were being created. On another easel were the sketches for a poster to advertise *The Penalty.* That was the title of the new Chaney movie. On another were sketches of costumes for another future Goldwyn film.

"This looks like a fun place to work," I said to my brothers. "It's much bigger than the one at Metropolitan Studios."

"Come on, J.W.!" Don shouted. "I think I see the publicity department!"

Don walked into the office where Papa worked. We found his desk, which had a nameplate sitting in front that read: "Conway Leo Gilclay, Assistant Director." Behind the desk were several theatrical posters for past Goldwyn Pictures productions starring Will Rogers and Mabel Normand, two of the studio's biggest stars.

Newspaper advertisements and articles from fan magazines were tacked to a bulletin board. On Papa's desk was the wedding picture Ma had sent to Goldwyn when they were hoping to become players at the studio. The "In" box was filled with magazines and newspapers in which Goldwyn films had been advertised or stars interviewed.

"Hey, this looks like a fun place to work, too," Don said. "I can see why Papa likes working here."

As soon as he said that, we heard someone else in the studio.

"Let's get out of here," Don whispered. "Maybe they do have a night watchman after all!"

We ran back through the studio to the back fence, past the art department, past the dressing rooms, past the sets.

"Stop!" we heard a voice say. "Didn't you see the sign?"

We didn't stop. We ran as fast as we could even though we

could hear the guard's footsteps behind us and see his flashlight beaming on the wall. Don helped Cliff and me over the fence first and then he hopped over. We ran back down the alley to Washington Boulevard. We almost got caught.

"That was a close call," Don said. "Let's get on home."

As we walked home to our apartment on Norton Drive, my mind was stuck on what I had seen in the art department at Goldwyn Pictures. It was much larger than the one at Metropolitan and was the first place in Hollywood that interested me.

"I'd sure like to work in the art department there," I said excitedly. "Mr. Granger said I was one of the best artists he had ever known."

"I thought you were going to go back to Texas and be a farmer," Don said, reminding me of my plan. I didn't think you'd ever back out on that idea."

"Well, a lot has happened since we left the farm in August. I know now that I can do a lot of things other than being a farmer like Grandpa," I explained. "At least I'd like to try the one I like best."

"All the men I've seen in Hollywood are sissies, J.W." Cliff said. "Do you want to work with a bunch of sissies?"

"I'm sure no dang sissy, Cliff, and you know it!" I yelled although it was the middle of the night.

"Then why do you sometimes sound like a girl?" Cliff teased because my voice had not yet changed like his.

"It's because I'm still a boy, you wimp!" I shouted as I hit him in the nose.

"Hey, you gave me a bloody nose!" Cliff shouted as I ran down the boulevard toward the beach. I heard Don tell Cliff not to follow me.

When I got to the beach, I sat and listened to the sound of the waves. I had not been there in several weeks. The beach was a good place to think and pray. During my first trip there, I had gotten quite sunburned under the arms and had to stay in bed for several days. I had fallen asleep on my back resting my head on my hands. It was a very unpleasant and embarrassing experience.

Tonight I just wanted to be away from my brothers and to think about my future. I would soon be fourteen and would be old enough to drive a car in California. I already had quite a few whiskers, and Papa said I would be shaving soon.

Since arriving in Hollywood, I had seen and done a lot related to the movie business. I had been an extra and was now working at a studio as an office boy where I got to see Harold Lloyd making a movie. I even got to visit the Beverly Hills home of a movie star, Norma Shearer, where Ma made her weekly delivery of flowers. Tonight I got to tour with my brothers the biggest and best studio in town.

All of these experiences had helped me to better understand what Hollywood was all about and the kinds of opportunities that were available for a young man like me. I knew now what I wanted to be. I wanted to be an artist!

When I was walking through the Goldwyn Pictures studio, I saw movie posters and title cards and sets and costumes being designed. It looked like a fun job to have, and I thought to myself, *I could do that!* Now I knew what Mr. Granger meant when he called California the "land of opportunity."

Before leaving the beach, I decided to talk to Mr. Burns about doing some jobs in the art department in addition to being just an office boy. I would take along my sketch pad that Ma gave me to show him what I can do. I was sure there was some way that I could use my talents as an artist in Hollywood.

I walked home feeling much better. The beach is a wonderful place to talk to God, and He really listens.

The sun was not yet up when I reached our apartment. Everyone was still asleep. I crawled in my bed without waking Sammy and Baby Juanita and went fast to sleep. It had been one of the best days of my life.

Sixteen

After school on Monday, I ran all the way to Metropolitan Studios to ask Mr. Burns about doing some work in the art department. Naturally I was winded when I got there and Mr. Burns let me catch my breath.

"What are you so excited about, J.W.?" Mr. Burns asked.

"I'd like to work in the art department," I exclaimed. "Do you think they've got anything for me to do there? I'm a pretty good artist. I even brought my sketch tablet to show them what I can do."

"Ready to move up already, are you?" Mr. Burns asked. "You're quite an ambitious young man."

"Well, yes, I am," I replied, "but it's not because I don't like working for you. You've been good to me. I'm just ready to see what I can do as an artist. I'm almost fourteen. Soon I'll be shaving and driving a car. I'm almost a man, Mr. Burns!"

"Yes, J.W., I know," Mr. Burns said. "I see those whiskers sprouting. I'll call the art director and see if he has anything that you can help him with."

Mr. Burns picked up his office phone and talked to the art director.

"J.W., our new office boy, is interested in working in the art department," Mr. Burns said. "Got anything he can do there?"

Mr. Burns frowned and then a wide smile appeared.

"That's a good idea, Tom. I'll let J.W. know," Mr. Burns said as he hung up the receiver.

"J.W., Tom doesn't have anything you could help him with now. You know we are a pretty small studio. But he had a good suggestion. There's a new company that just opened down the street. They print theatrical posters. It's called the Southern Poster Company. Tom says they could use some people to help silkscreen posters. He says the pay is pretty good, too. He even gave me the number of the manager to call."

"Sounds great!" I replied.

"I'll call the manager," Mr. Burns said, "and see if they can use you. It may not be exactly what you had in mind. You'd be printing posters rather than designing them, but it's a start."

"It sure is," I said.

Mr. Burns dialed the number and was soon talking to the manager.

"I've got a hard-working young office boy over here who's ready to assume more responsibility. He wants to work in our art department, but we don't have anything for him to do. Tom Gibson, our art director, thought you might be able to use him. How about it?"

Mr. Burns smiled broadly as he hung up the phone and came around to the other side of the desk and shook my hand. "The manager says to come over so he can interview you. He wants to see some of your drawings. He may be able to use you in designing posters as well as printing. J.W.," he said. "I'll miss you, but I don't want to stand in your way. He's working on the poster for the new Lon Chaney movie which opens this weekend. Why don't you deliver today's mail and then go on over? If he decides you're not the right boy for the job, you can come on back."

"I'll miss you, too, Mr. Burns," I said with a big smile, "but I really appreciate your helping me get a new job as an artist. I'll let you know what happens."

When I got to the Southern Poster Company, the manager showed me the Lon Chaney poster that he was printing. Mr. Chaney was standing on his stumps holding himself up with crutches. "He looks like his legs have been cut off," I said. "It's incredible!"

"It sure is," the manager said. "Now let me see some of your drawings."

I pulled out my tablet in which I had drawn lots of pictures of my farm in Texas and a few of the Hollywood scenery which Ma thought was so beautiful. The manager looked at each page carefully and then gave me the tablet back to me.

"You're a talented young man, J.W.," he said. "You have a natural ability to draw—especially landscapes, but I don't think you are quite ready to design posters for movies. I'd recommend you take an art course at school where you can learn more about drawing and design and get more practice."

"But one of my bosses in Texas said I was one of the best artists he had ever seen," I said in a disappointed voice.

"You are a good artist, J.W.," the manager said. "No doubt about it. You just need more training to use your talent in designing posters. But I can still use you right now to print them. How 'bout it? Can you give me a couple hours of work before dinner?"

"Sure can," I said, "and I'm going to sign up for an art course in the spring."

That night at dinner, I could tell that Papa was really excited.

"The new Chaney movie is finished," Papa said, "and Mr. Goldwyn says that all the studio employees can bring their families to the premiere. He'll be in New York for the premiere there, but Sam has talked Lon Chaney into making a public appearance at the Hollywood opening since it's his first movie for us. Isn't that great! I told you he'd probably be there, J.W."

"It sure is, Papa," I said. "You can count on me to join you."

"How about the rest of you?" Papa asked. "You can invite Sally, Don."

"Sure," Don said., "I'm not a Chaney fan, but I've wanted to go to a premiere."

"Me, too," Cliff inserted. "All we have been to have been some sneak previews at our theater for some new Tom Mix movies. This should really be fun."

"Then it's all set," Papa said. "I'll let my boss know that I'd like to use one of the studio cars on Saturday night. We will have to be there about an hour early to be sure the radio and newspaper people get some materials that my department has prepared."

"I've got some good news, too," I said with a big grin. "I've got a new job. I told Mr. Burns that I had decided to become an artist and asked him if he thought there might be something I could do in the art department. He called the art director, but he had nothing. He recommended a new company down the street that is printing theatrical posters for new movies. It's the Southern Poster Company."

"Hey," Papa said, "they're doing the one for the new Chaney film."

"I know," I replied. "I helped the manager print it this afternoon. It's terrific!"

"I saw the design done by our art department, but I haven't seen the actual poster," Papa replied. "I'm very proud of you, son. What made you decide on being an artist instead of a farmer?"

When I started to answer, I realized that it was the night that we climbed over the fence and went into the Goldwyn studio without him knowing it. I looked at Don for some advice. I had mentioned to him that the art department looked like a fun place to work. I kicked him under the table.

"Papa," Don responded. "I think I know when it happened. You know how we were bugging you to go on a tour of your studio and you were too busy?"

"Yeah, I remember," Papa said.

"Well, I convinced J.W. and Cliff to go with me one night on a tour of the studio," Don confessed.

"How'd you get in?" Papa asked. "They have a night watchman there who guards the front gate."

"We crawled over the back fence," Don said.

"Oh, no!" Papa replied. "The guard mentioned there had been some intruders last weekend, but he said there had been no damage to anything."

"That's right, Papa," I said. "We didn't damage anything. We just walked up to your office and then back. That's when I went into the art department and saw all the swell things they do there."

"I don't want you to do anything like that again, boys," Papa said sternly. "I didn't know how anxious you were for a tour. After the premiere, I'll take you all—even Baby Juanita. Okay?"

"Okay!" all the boys shouted.

I thought Saturday night would never come. I told my friend Bill what we were going to do, but he was the only one I told. I didn't want the other boys at the lunch table to think that I was bragging about seeing Lon Chaney.

Papa had driven the car home from the studio on Friday night so our transportation was all set. Don and Cliff made arrangements for their shifts at the theater to be covered by two friends. Saturday afternoon, we all took baths and washed our hair. Ma let Baby Juanita wear some of her new perfume and Papa let all of the boys have a few spashes of aftershave lotion. My family had never smelled so good.

Mrs. Malloy had helped Ma find a used clothing store where she was able to purchase "new" clothes for all the children. She even got ties for the boys. We really looked spiffy!

On the way to the theater, we picked up Sally at the boarding house. Papa told us that the New York premiere had gone smoothly and that the reviews had been excellent. "One newspaper said That *The Miracle Man* had made Lon Chaney a star, but *The Penalty* confirms his new status!" Papa shouted. "Some review, huh?"

When we got to the theater, crowds were already forming in front. Papa drove our car around to the back of the theater, and we walked through the alley to where several radio stations had set up microphones. Papa's boss had come down with a bad cold, so Papa was in charge of everything.

"Hi, guys," Papa said to the radio and newspaper reporters who were covering the event. "I've got a release for you about the movie. It also tells a bit about Lon Chaney and his co-star, Claire Adams. They should be here within the hour."

"Does it give us the plot of the movie?" one of the reporters asked. "I understand it's different than the book."

"That's right," Papa said. "The screenwriters made a few changes, especially in the ending, but I don't want to give away any surprises. I hope you guys are planning to stay and see it. Chaney gives an incredible performance. I've already viewed it twice and you'd swear he'd cut off his legs for this part. I've never seen anything like it."

About the time that Papa was distributing the press releases, a big black limousine pulled up in front of the theater and the crowd screamed.

"It's Claire!" one man yelled.

Claire Adams, escorted by a lesser-known actor in the movie, emerged from the limousine and waved to the crowd. Flashbulbs popped as the photographers took pictures.

"Isn't she beautiful?" Don said. I've never seen her in a movie before."

"This is her first movie with Lon Chaney," I said, "but I think she has been acting for years, waiting to be discovered, just like Sally."

Claire Adams moved elegantly up to where the microphones were placed and was interviewed by the radio reporters there. She then went into the theater to take her seat.

The theater manager welcomed her and pointed out where the cast would be sitting.

"I hope Mr. Chaney is here soon," Papa said to me.

"Lon! Lon!" came a woman's scream from the crowd. More flashbulbs popped.

"He's here," Papa said.

A shiny white convertible pulled up, and in it was Lon Chaney and his wife, Hazel, and his son, Creighton. Mr. Chaney did look like my uncle in Texas! The resemblance was incredible. He was a stocky, slightly bald man of about thirty-seven years. He smiled broadly and waved at the crowd. He let his wife and son out of the car first. His son looked like he was about my age and really favored his father.

Lon Chaney and his family moved over the red carpet up to the microphones where they answered a few questions. Then Mr. Chaney saw Papa and went up to him and shook his hand.

"I've got my whole family here tonight, Mr. Chaney," Papa said, "and I told them I would introduce you to them."

While his wife and son stood by, Lon Chaney shook each of our hands, even Baby Juanita's. I wanted to say something to him, but for the first time in my life, I was speechless. I think he could tell what a fan I was by how vigorously I shook his hand. At least I hope he knew.

After the movie had been screened and the lights went back on, the audience gave Mr. Chaney a standing ovation. Although his character was a criminal, he had only turned to crime after his legs had been needlessly amputated by a surgeon following an accident. He finally gets the surgeon to graft new legs onto his stumps, but after the operation, he is killed by a former associate in crime. Practically everyone was in tears at the end of the movie, including me.

Papa said goodbye to the theater manager and thanked him for his help.

"That was a fine premiere, Mr. Gilclay," the manager said. "I'll let your boss know how smoothly everything went. Sorry Roy was under the weather."

We then walked to our car and got in.

"Well, what did you think?" Papa asked. "Wasn't that something?"

"It really was," I said. "I still can't believe I met Lon Chaney."

"Me neither," Cliff chimed in.

"We all had a great time, Conway," Ma said. "Thanks for inviting us."

"How about ice cream sundaes at Joe's hot dog stand—my treat?" I asked.

"Sounds great," Papa said, "but what about your trip to Texas?"

"I've decided to put it off and give Hollywood a chance," I replied. "That's why I want to do something special for my family tonight."

As my family and Sally sat around the same table at the restaurant where we had eaten our first hot dogs just a few months before, my feelings were quite different. I had never been so happy. My family's move to Hollywood was turning out to be just as good as Mr. Granger had said it would be.

I still needed to write Grandpa about my decision, but I knew he would understand. I'd also write Joseph and draw him a picture of the Southern Poster Company building. I am good at drawing landscapes and buildings.

Soon we would be celebrating Thanksgiving, and we sure had lots to be thankful for—especially me, the budding artist in the Gilclay family.

Printed in the United States
34627LVS00002B/4-51

9 781413 753783